Maddy Madison
and the
CRAZY CARNIVAL

A Quilters Club Mystery

(Book 20)

Marjory Sorrell
Rockwell

Maddy Madison
and the
CRAZY CARNIVAL

A Quilters Club Mystery

ABSOLUTELY AMA⚡ING eBOOKS

Habent Sua Fata Libelli

ABSOLUTELY AMAZING eBOOKS

Manhanset House
Shelter Island Hts., New York 11965-0342

bricktower@aol.com • tech@absolutelyamazingebooks.com
• absolutelyamazingebooks.com

The Absolutely Amazing eBooks colophon is a trademark of
J. T. Colby & Company, Inc.

Library of Congress Cataloging-in-Publication Data
Rockwell, Marjory Sorrell.
Maddy Madison and the Crazy Carnival #20.
p. cm.
    1. FICTION / Mystery & Detective / Amateur Sleuth.
    2. FICTION / Mystery & Detective / General.
    3. CRAFTS & HOBBIES/ Quilts & Quilting.
Fiction, I. Title.
ISBN: 978-1-955036-71-9, Trade Paper

May 2024

Quilter Club Mysteries

Quilters Club Mysteries

By Marjory Sorrell Rockwell

The Quilter's Club Quartet (Anthology 1)
The Quilter's Club Trio (Anthology 2)
The Quilter's Club Triple Stack (Anthology 3)
The Quilter's Club Threefold (Anthology 4)

The Underhanded Stitch (Book 1)
The Patchwork Puzzler (Book 2)
Coming Unraveled (Book 3)
Hemmed In (Book 4)
Sewed Up Tight (Book 5)
All Tangled Up (Book 6)
A Christmas Quilt (Prequel – Book 7)
Needled (Book 8)
Stitch In Time (Book 9)

Cross Stitch (Book 10)
Fat Quarters (Book 11)
Stitch in the Ditch (Book 12)
Quilt Block (Book 13)
A Thimbleful of Murder (Book 14)
Sew Be It (Book 15)
Stab Stitching and Other Dangers (Book 16)
A Golden Needle and a Silver Bullet (Book 17)
A Backstitch Murder (Book 18)
Quilting On A Midsummer's Night (Book 19)
Maddy Madison and the Crazy Carnival (Book 20)

Available from
AbsolutelyAmazingEbooks.com

When life gives you scraps,

make a quilt...

Table of Contents

Introduction..11

Chapter One: Welcome to the Crazy Carnival...............13

Chapter Two: Meet the Quilters Club...........................15

Chapter Three: Barffy the Clown................................20

Chapter Four: Aggie Checks In....................................23

Chapter Five: Cecelia LaToya Jackson.........................28

Chapter Six: A New Candidate Comes Forward...........31

Chapter Seven: Murder, He Wrote..............................34

Chapter Eight: Small Town Politics.............................38

Chapter Nine: Maddy's Summit Meeting.....................41

Chapter Ten: Asking Permission ... kinda...................44

Chapter Eleven: Crazy Quilts......................................46

Chapter Twelve: Doc Medford....................................50

Chapter Thirteen: Birdie Longstreet...........................53

Chapter Fourteen: Col. Oscar Owensby.......................56

Chapter Fifteen: Littleton & Co...................................60

Chapter Sixteen: The Clown Car.................................63

Chapter Seventeen: The Juggling Juggernauts............66

Chapter Eighteen: The History of Clowns....................69

Chapter Nineteen: The Fake Colonel...........................72

Chapter Twenty: The Lost Boy....................................75

Chapter Twenty-One: Grammy's Undercover Agent.....78

Chapter Twenty-Two: The False Winner......................81

Chapter Twenty-Three: Circus Clowns............................83

Chapter Twenty-Four: Bad News.....................................87

Chapter Twenty-Five: Evil Clowns.................................89

Chapter Twenty-Six: Such a Nice Lady..........................93

Chapter Twenty-Seven: The Second Tox Report...........96

Chapter Twenty-Eight: What Was the Motive?............101

Chapter Twenty-Nine: The Prodigal Son Returns........105

Chapter Thirty: The Great Debate................................109

Chapter Thirty-One: Back to School.............................113

Chapter Thirty-Two: Slight-of-Hand............................118

Chapter Thirty-Three: Fright Night.............................121

Chapter Thirty-Four: The DNA Results........................125

Chapter Thirty-Five: No Nuptials.................................131

Chapter Thirty-Six: A Redo...135

Chapter Thirty-Seven: Green Hair and Ham................139

Chapter Thirty-Eight: Slow Start.................................143

Chapter Thirty-Nine: "They're All Scary!"...................146

Chapter Forty: A Visit to Information Central.............148

Chapter Forty-One: Clown Show...................................153

Chapter Forty-Two: Couples Night...............................158

Chapter Forty-Three: More About Maddy.....................162

Chapter Forty-Four: Sprinkles the Clown.....................165

Chapter Forty-Five: Oxymoron.....................................168

Chapter Forty-Six: The Poison......................................170

Chapter Forty-Seven: The Second Debate.....................179

Chapter Forty-eight: A New Round of Interviews.......183

Chapter Forty-Nine: Maddy's Family Visit...................189

Chapter Fifty: Three Eyes...191

Chapter Fifty-One: Swami Bombay and his Elephant.195

Chapter Fifty-Two: The Car Wreck...............................199

Chapter Fifty-Three: Not an Accident..........................201

Chapter Fifty-Four: The Flying Floyds..........................205

Chapter Fifty-Five: Out-of-Towner...............................209

Chapter Fifty-Six: The Timeline...................................212

Chapter Fifty-Seven: Wrapping It Up..........................216

Chapter Fifty-Eight: Confession..................................220

Chapter Fifty-Nine: Bobby Ray's Big Lie....................222

Chapter Sixty: Election Day...225

Epilogue...228

About the Author...232

Maddy's New Website..233

INTRODUCTION

This being the 20th book in the Quilters Club series, I ask myself if it should be the last. Readers have followed Maddy Madison and her family through mystery after mystery, murder after murder. Followers have watched as her granddaughter Aggie grew up, as family secrets were unveiled, as the Hoople Quadruplets were exposed, as that Tornado nearly wiped out the little town of Caruthers Corners, as Maddy and her husband Beau moved into the big mansion on the hill and back to their Victorian home on Melon Pickers Row. It's been quite a saga.

I think I'll let you readers decide.

Or maybe I'll leave it up to the characters.

Maddy and Aggie have a mind of their own.

-Marjory Sorrell Rockwell

CHAPTER ONE

Welcome to the Crazy Carnival

Last Fall, Maddy Madison and her pals at the Quilters Club sewed an elaborate 88-inch x 88-inch Pictorial Quilt, the colorful strips of fabric depicting a carnival scene with red-and-yellow tents, a golden carousel with circling horses, and a tall Ferris Wheel loaded with waving children and smiling parents standing below.

This handmade quilt was scheduled to be auctioned off at the Caruthers Corners Crazy Carnival. Backed by the Town Council, this new event was designed to raise awareness for the small town (pop. 2,312) and attract more visitors to this northeastern corner of Indiana.

As you may know, Maddy's husband Beau currently serves as president of the 8-person Town Council. And their son-in-law Mark Tidemore is Caruthers Corner's popular two-term mayor.

Gimble & Gimble – a big-league PR firm out of Indianapolis – had been engaged to help the town pull it off. When Beau suggested the carnival idea, G&G had jumped on board, making it their own. Before you could say "Barnum & Bailey!" the large Town Square had been turned into a circus grounds with twinkling lights and peaked canvas tents and rattling amusement park rides with the bouncy music of a steam-whistle calliope echoing in the background.

The Caruthers Corners Crazy Carnival was a bit of a patchwork itself: The rides were courtesy of Anderson Amusements, a familiar traveling show in the Midwest; the animals came from the local Haney Bros. Zoo & Exotic Animal Refuge; and the high-wire act was none other than the Flying Floyd Family. (Legendary aerialist Jason Jonathan Floyd had been born near here, just like James Dean, Steve McQueen, Axl Rose, Vivaca A. Fox, and David Letterman ... to list a few Hoosier celebrities).

The Carnival's sideshow was uniquely homegrown – populated by the inhabitants of Crackleton Crossing. Located just north of town, this community had been written up in the annals of the Baltimore Geographic Society for its historic consanguinity. These local oddities included giants, dwarfs, ectrodactyl-handed lobster boys, a hypertrichotic wolfman, microcephalic pinheads, conjoined twins, and even a weird-looking guy with three eyes.

Clowns, of course, were plentiful. A professional entertainment booker out of Chicago supplied a clown car stuffed with 12 bozos of all stripes, sizes, shapes, and colors. Maddy's son Freddie – now the town's fire chief – reprised his popular role as Sparkplug the Fire Prevention Clown, the greasepaint hiding his many burn scars.

Everything was going quite well. That is, until Barffy the Red-Nosed Clown dropped dead in the center ring on opening night.

CHAPTER TWO

Meet the Quilters Club

With the success of Caruthers Corners' recent summer promotions – in particular, an open-air production of Shakespeare's *A Midsummer Night's Dream* – the Town Council had been looking for a new event in the Fall. Beau Madison suggested a carnival. After all, the town already had a Ferris wheel at the back of the Town Square, over there just beyond the gazebo and the koi pond, almost at the edge of the Pleasant Meadows church property. Rides were only 25¢. Not exactly as impressive as the London Eye, the Wonder Wheel in Coney Island, or the Big O in Japan, but a nice touch for a small hamlet in Indiana.

This was a perfect venue for a carnival, a fundraiser that would feature an amalgam of local folks and traveling carnies and professional circus acts. That ought to attract visitors from Ohio and Chicago and points beyond.

The Town Council voted to do it 8 to 0.

Thus launched the Caruthers Corners Crazy Carnival. Everybody was having a good time – until Barffy the Clown died under mysterious circumstances. Nobody could ascertain the cause of death. Police Chief Jim Purdue was at a loss. The Indiana State Police were mystified. Was it foul play ... or a heart attack as Doc Medford put on the Death Certificate?

The question at hand, was this going to be a case for Maddy and her Quilters Club pals?

~ ~ ~

If you've followed Maddy Madison's adventures, you know the Quilters Club – Maddy, Lizzie, Cookie, and Bootsie – have an impressive reputation as amateur sleuths. Having solved a number of local mysteries, many people thought of them as quasi-detectives. Sometimes Maddy's grandchildren got in the act, but they were away at school now. That left it up to – as the *Burpyville Gazette* had dubbed them – that "marvelous quartet of Miss Marples."

You wouldn't think there'd be much crime in a sleepy little town like Caruthers Corners, but the gals had tackled everything from murders to mysterious disappearances, buried gold to hidden Viking treasures. Just ask anybody about the Lost Boys or the Beasley Ghost or the thieves who stole Captain Perricock's antediluvian fossil collection.

Maddy was married to Beauregard Hollingsworth Madison IV, a direct descendant of one of the Town Founders. That was a big deal in these parts. In 1827, Jacob Caruthers, Ferdinand Jinks, and Col. Beauregard Madison were leading a wagon train West when it broke down on the banks of the Wabash River. The town sprang up here despite battles with local Potawatomi Indians and disputes among the settlers.

You can see the Founders' statues near the bandstand in the grassy Town Square. Col. Madison is the one that looks like that lanky *Pig in the City* actor, James Cromwell. The other two looked like extras from *The Wild Bunch*.

If you've ever met Maddy, you'd know she's a pleasant oval-faced woman with silvery hair. In her mid-60s, she might be a few pounds overweight, but not so much as you'd notice.

She sometimes samples too many of her watermelon cookies and slices of watermelon upside-down cake.

Maddy was the de facto leader of the Quilters Club. Over the years its members had dwindled down to her three bestest pals. And the kids.

Lizzie Ridenour was by far the better quilter, a multi-term state champion. These days Lizzie served as director of the Hoople Quilting Heritage Museum. Her husband Edgar was a retired bank president who spent his spare time fishing on the Wabash. And he had plenty of spare time.

Cookie Bentley headed the Caruthers Corners Historical Society, that non-profit occupying a wing of the Perricock Museum of Science & History. Her husband Ben was the largest landowner in the entire county.

Bootsie Purdue had founded Strays & Others, the local animal rescue. An ardent dog-lover, she has almost as many animals at home as at the shelter. Her hubby Jim (as noted above) is the police chief, although he was again threatening to retire. Handing out parking tickets was boring, and what little crime the town saw was often solved – to Jim's great chagrin – by the Quilters Club.

Burpyville Gazette, the biggest – no, you can make that the only – newspaper in the county, recently had this to say about the Quilters Club:

> SEPTEMBER – Over in Caruthers Corners, a quartet of would-be Agatha Christies has gained quite a track record for solving crimes, big and small. Readers may recall that incident when the four women thwarted a

madman trying to poison the area's water supply. Or when they uncovered a meth lab in the middle of town. Or that time they discovered a buried wagon-load of gold. Or more recently when they nabbed the dognappers who took Mrs. Wade Simonton's prize-winning Cockadoodle.

Believe it or not, this little quilting bee also sews patchwork quilts – Amish Star Crossed Quilts, Nine-Patches, Double Wedding Rings, and traditional Log Cabins. Headed up by Madelyn Madison, it calls itself the Quilters Club. Members include Katherine Bentley, Elizabeth Ridenour, and Barbara Jo Purdue.

Now the four women have created a large Pictorial Quilt that shows the Caruthers Corners Crazy Carnival in all its colorful glory. And it can be yours if you hold the winning number.

The drawing got postponed due to the sudden death of Walter Bradford – better known in the circus world as Barffy the Red-Nosed Clown.

A drawing by Mayor Mark Tidemore picked a winning number. And here it is:

756F9K

If you hold this ticket, contact the Caruthers Corners Mayor's Office to collect your Crazy Carnival Pictorial Quilt. It is sure to become a collector's item.

CHAPTER THREE

Barffy the Clown

Walter Ambrose Bradford had been born in Boston to a show biz family in 1950. His father was a fondly-remembered Vaudeville performer known as Bendable Brad, the Human Pretzel. His mother Florence had been a street mime, popular for her "trapped in an invisible box" routine.

At 12, Walt ran away from home to – literally – join the circus. Working as a roustabout, he eventually moved from traveling carnivals in the Midwest to the Ringling Bros. and Barnum & Baily Circus. That's the Big Time in the world of Big Tops.

Billed as The Greatest Show on Earth, the circus toured from 1871 to 2017. (Note: Barnum & Bailey's Greatest Show on Earth, a circus created by P.T. Barnum and James Anthony Baily, merged with the Ringling Bros. World's Greatest Shows in 1919.)

However, with diminishing attendance and high operating costs, the circus performed its final show on May 21, 2017 ... although current owners announced that the circus would resume touring in the fall of 2023, but without animals.

For its grand re-opening, Barffy the Red-Nosed Clown had been booked to return to the Ringling Bros. center ring. Now, that wouldn't be happening.

~ ~ ~

Thanks to a chance meeting with Emmett Kelly back in the '70s, circus roustabout Walter Bradford made the decision to become a clown.

Emmett Leo Kelly was famous for his hobo character, Weary Willie. A one-time trapeze artist, Kelly had sometimes filled in as a clown at Howe's Great London Circus. With the popularity of Willie growing, he'd given up the high wire for greasepaint.

Emmett Kelly had worked for the Sells-Floto and Hagenbeck-Wallace circuses until 1931 and then for Cole Bros Circus. (Cole Bros. billed him as "the world's funniest clown.") In 1942, Kelly joined Ringling Bros. and Barnum & Baily, and remained a featured act there until the late '50s.

Kelly was inducted into the International Clown Hall of Fame in 1989, the International Circus Hall of Fame in 1994, and the Hall of Famous Missourians at the Missouri State Capitol in 1998.

Walt Bradford thought making people laugh – like Emmett Kelly did – was a better career path than sweeping up elephant dung and raising tents. Being a roustabout paid little better than room and board, while a clown's salary averaged about $36,000 a year. That sounded like good money to him.

Emmett Kelly encouraged Walt. "But you'll need a gimmick," the elderly clown advised him. For Kelly, it had been the sad hobo schtick. So Walt built his character around a big red nose. He got the idea from that old Christmas song, "Rudolph the Red-Nosed Reindeer." He'd always liked the Gene Autry recording of it.

In 1981, Walter Bradford graduated from the Ringling Bros. and Barnum & Bailey Clown College. After that, his career took off. Barffy the Red-Nose Clown became a featured performer at Ringling Bros. Patrons laughed and slapped their knees when he wandered about the ring, sniffing at elephants' butts and unicycle seats and audience members' armpits. He wished he'd called himself Sniffy.

When Ringling Bros. closed down in 2017, Walt started playing county fairs and small carnivals. Marking time until Feld Entertainment brought the circus back to coliseums and sports stadiums and other indoor arenas next year.

Now 72, Barffy moved a little slower; but his comic timing was intact. He had just started his act in the main tent at the Caruthers Corners Crazy Carnival – sniffing around the onlookers, spraying perfume into the air, staggering about and pretending to be dizzy – when he suddenly grunted, grabbed at his throat, gasped several times and then collapsed. Most thought it was part of the act.

Doc Medford opined that Walter Ambrose Bradford was dead before he hit the sawdust.

CHAPTER FOUR

Aggie Checks In

Maddy's granddaughter Aggie – she was the elder daughter of Tilly and Mark Tidemore – phoned that weekend. She had a favor to ask.

Typical.

Aggie was in pre-law at Yale, following in her father's footsteps. Before becoming the town's mayor, her dad had been a high-powered attorney known in legal circles as "Mark the Shark."

Blonde and blue-eyed, with a light sprinkling of freckles across her nose, Agnes Madelyn Tidemore was turning into an attractive young woman. Boys buzzed about like bees in search of honey, but with her studies she didn't have time to date. What's more, she was kinda going steady with a boy back home – though she didn't consider it really serious.

She missed Caruthers Corners, but was building a large group of friends in New Haven. And she was on the Dean's List. Things were going well. If she'd been a boy, she'd likely have been inducted into the Skull and Bones. Her dad had been a Bonesman, not that he would talk about it. A secret society was a secret society, after all.

Despite Aggie's growing number of friends, at the top of the list remained her 17-year-old cousin N'yen – an Advanced Placement student studying astrophysics at Northwestern –

and her BFF Sissy Jackson – who was finishing her senior year at Caruthers High. This trio was considered junior members of the Quilters Club. They had helped solve a number of mysteries along with the mainstay adult quartet.

However, this phone call had nothing to do with Barffy the Clown's unexplained death. To Maddy's surprise, Aggie was calling about her dog.

Tige, a cute little long-haired dachshund mix, was getting up there in dog years. When Aggie went off to college, Tige had come to live with Maddy and Beau. He reminded Maddy of the dog she'd had as a child, named after Buster Brown's dog who lived in a shoe.

Maddy still remembered the shoe company's slogan:

"I'm Buster Brown.
"I live in a shoe.
"That's my dog Tige.
"Look for him there, too."

The shoe company was still in business, but now it's called Caleres – owner of Naturalizer and Dr. Scholl's, among other brands.

~ ~ ~

"I'm thinking of getting an apartment off campus," Aggie said to her grandmother. "One that would let me have a pet. What would you think of Tige coming out here to live with me?"

"Oh my. We would miss that little rascal. But he's your dog. We'd miss him, like we miss you ... and N'yen."

N'yen Madison was the adopted son of Bill Madison, Maddy's firstborn who now ran an NGO children's center in Chicago. Bill and Kathy were do-gooders. A certified genius,

N'yen was enrolled in Northwestern's graduate school even though he was only a teenager. Last year he'd been included in *Forbes'* 30 Under 30 list of "young people who are changing the world."

Maddy and Beau had three children – Bill, Tilly, and Freddie. And they doted on their six grandchildren. But Aggie and N'yen were closest to Maddy's heart. Maybe it was because they, along with their friend Sissy (as Cecelia Jackson was known) were off-and-on members of the Quilters Club.

Turns out, Aggie did have questions about Barffy. "While I've got you on the phone," Aggie continued without pause, "what's the scoop on that dead clown. Anything there for the Quilters Club?"

"Doubtful," replied her grandmother. "Doc Medford says it was a heart attack."

"Just as well. I'd hate to miss out on a juicy murder case. I won't be home till the Christmas holidays."

"Count your blessings that crime is at a low ebb here in Caruthers Corners. Last case we had was a missing dog, that Cockadoodle who got lost chasing Maisie's cat, Alexander the Great."

"I'm happy to have sat that one out," giggled Aggie. "Where did you find the dog?"

"Wandering out near Green Scum Pond. Covered in icky mud, but otherwise fine, his tail wagging."

"I'd put my money on Alexander any day. He's a tough ol' feline."

"Yes, indeed. We think the cat deliberately lured the dog out to the pond, then left him there. He's a crafty one."

"The *Burpyville Gazette* said it was dognappers ...?" She subscribed to the digital edition.

"A dognapper that prefers Fancy Feast tuna," laughed Maddy. "The *Gazette* sometimes gets its facts slightly twisted."

"Green Scum Pond, that's four or five blocks from the diner." Alexander lived behind Cozy Café. Maddy's fraternal twin Maisie Walters – owner of the diner – swore the cat wasn't hers, but try telling that to Alexander!

"Yes, Alexander led that Cockadoodle on a merry chase."

"Poor pooch. I'll bet he was glad to get home."

Maddy cautiously changed the subject. "The mayoral election is coming up. Looks like your Dad will be running unopposed again."

"Too bad I won't be there to help put up campaign signs. But I suppose there's no need to bother. It's more a tradition than a necessity. Everybody knows my daddy."

"True," smiled Maddy. "He got 98% of the vote last time around."

"He likes being mayor."

Maddy switched gears again. "If you get an apartment in time, you can take Tige back with you when you come home over Christmas."

"Okay. I miss that little hound dog." She was parsing his breed; *dachshund* translated as "badger hound." Not that Tige had ever encountered a badger in his entire wiener-dog life.

"Did you hear about Sissy? She was a hit in the school play."

"Yes, *The Sound of Music*. That girl's got a set of pipes on her. I hear N'yen came home to catch the performance." Her cousin and her best friend were still an item. Going steady. Or semi-engaged. Or something like that.

"That's right, he did. It was good to see him."

"Wish I could have been there. But N'yen has an advantage, Northwestern being about 500 miles closer than Yale."

"Sissy misses you guys. She hangs out here at the house 'most every day. Eats with us several days a week. We may as well add her to our list of grandchildren. N'yen and Freddie's daughter Donna Ann are adopted. What's one more?"

"If anything happens to her grandfather, I suspect you'll get her for real." Buck Jackson was Sissy's legal guardian, her mother lost in the drug rehab system in Alabama. Buck was Beau Madison's old Army buddy; they had served together in Vietnam, surviving the Lam Son 719 offensive and other skirmishes back in the early '70s. Ironic that her Grampy wound up with an adopted Vietnamese grandson. They were great fishing buddies.

"Probably so. Buck would want us to look after her."

"Tell her I said 'hey' ..."

"Tell her yourself. I hear her coming in the front door right now."

CHAPTER FIVE

Cecelia LaToya Jackson

"I won!" Sissy Jackson announced grandly. You could hear the excitement in her voice.

"Won what?" asked Aggie, holding the phone close to her ear. Her Grammy had just put her BFF on the line.

"The drawing for the quilt. I have the winning ticket right here in my hand. Number 756F9K, just like in the newspaper."

"Congratulations, girlfriend. Does Grammy know yet?"

"No. I just walked in the door and she handed me the phone."

"I hope there's no conflict of interest."

"What kind of conflict?"

"You know, practically being a member of the family."

"But technically, I'm not. So I want my quilt. Gonna hang it on the wall of my bedroom. That way, every night will be a carnival. Who do I contact to collect on my winning ticket?"

"My daddy, I'd guess. He's the guy in charge."

Not only had Mayor Mark Tidemore overseen the Crazy Carnival, but he had been the one to pick the winning ticket in the drawing for the Pictorial Quilt.

"Yeah, your dad was quite the ringmaster. You should've seen him in that red-and-blue split-tail suit and fancy top hat."

"Mom emailed me a picture. He looked like Hugh Jackman in *The Greatest Showman*."

"You dad is one cool dude," agreed Sissy. "I can't wait to turn in my winning ticket to him."

~ ~ ~

Birdie Longstreet called 9-1-1. She got one of the Dobbler sisters, the two siblings who maintained the police department's switchboard in ever-confusing shifts.

"What's the nature of your emergency," said Myrtle in a bored voice. She recognized the number as belonging to Beatrice Longstreet, a ditzy old lady with a vivid imagination. She was always reporting sightings of Elvis, Bigfoot, and Little Green Men. Not a victim of Alzheimer's, just born with a few screws loose.

"My life was threatened by a clown," stated Birdie.

"And where did this happen?"

"Friday night at the circus. Where else would I meet up with a clown?"

Myrtle sighed. "How did he threaten your life?" She knew many people were frightened by clowns with their garish makeup and phantasmagorical costumes. In Birdie's befuddled state of mind, she could easily have interpreted that as imminent danger.

"He said, 'Get out of here or I will cut your throat.'"

"Get out of where?"

"One of the dressing rooms at the circus. I was trying to find a restroom and took a wrong turn."

Myrtle knew the old woman was easily confused. "So you walked in on one of the clowns getting dressed?"

"No, no. He was already in full makeup. He was upset that I caught him writing something on the dressing room mirror. That's when he threatened to cut my throat. It was most scary."

"Which clown was it?" Myrtle dutifully wrote down the details on the Call Report form.

"How would I know. All I can tell you is that he had green hair."

"Alright, I will pass this complaint along to Chief Purdue. I'm sure he'll look into it," said the dispatcher.

"Thank you, Elvina."

"It's Myrtle. Elvina's got the night shift this week."

CHAPTER SIX

A New Candidate Comes Forward

To everyone's surprise, Ken Wurgler announced he was running for mayor. A skinny nervous man with a bad toupee, Wurgler headed up the local Chamber of Commerce. It was a one-man office, his main duty being to work with the mayor and Town Council to develop pro-business initiatives. The Caruthers Corners Crazy Carnival had been one of these.

His entry in the race came at the last minute. The election was already upon them. The Town Council had to reprint the ballots to get Wurgler's name on them.

The town's bylaws had no mayoral term limit, so everybody had assumed Mark Tidemore was good for a third four-year term. His run as mayor had been unopposed until now.

"What the heck do you think you're doing?" demanded Edgar Ridenour. The former bank president sat on the Town Council along with Ken Wurgler. He and Ben Bentley were squeezed into a corner booth with Wurgler at the Cozy Café having an unofficial "backroom" meeting.

The head of the Chamber of Commerce looked defiant. "Mark Tidemore bungled the Crazy Carnival – what with that clown dying. And there was a nasty death during this summer's presentation of *A Midsummer Night's Dream.* Somebody needs to manage these thing better."

"And you're the guy?"

"Well, I did organize that successful business conference last year. Nobody died there."

"*Pshaw!*" guffawed Edgar. "That was twelve local businessmen giving a presentation at Caruthers High's job fair."

"We placed thirty-two students in jobs upon graduation."

"Serving creamy whip at the Dairy Queen is not considered a big career choice," said Edgar.

"We placed two teller trainees at the Caruthers Corners Savings and Loan," Ken Wurgler said defensively. "You should appreciate that."

"Yes, I recall. One quit after the first month. The second was caught stealing money from the till."

"That was unfortunate."

Ben Bentley spoke up. "Look, Mark Tidemore has done a great job as mayor. The way he rebuilt the town after the 2018 Northeastern Indiana Tornado will long be remembered."

Wurgler looked like he'd swallowed a lemon. His thick eyebrows met like dueling caterpillars. His rat-brown toupee had slipped slightly off center. "Credit should go to the Caruthers Corners Restoration Coalition, the fund set up by the Hoople family."

"Aren't you forgetting, Mark's wife is a member of the Hoople family?" interjected Edgar. "She and Mark lived up there on the hill in the Hoople Mansion before the old ladies died in that car accident and the heirs donated the mansion to the town as a retirement home. Mark had a hand in that."

"Yeah, yeah. But I have the backing of local businesses. N.L. Purdue is my cousin. His EZ Seat Chair Factory is the largest employer in this town. That's a lot of voters."

"Newcomb Lamont Purdue's brother Bobby Ray is a big supporter of Mark Tidemore," said Ben. "And I'd remind you that Bobby Ray's even richer than his brother."

"But he doesn't employ anyone. Protecting jobs, that's what this is all about. Dead clowns scare away tourists, hurt employment."

"Don't you think you're stretching the point," replied Edgar.

"Not in the least. Matter of fact, that's going to be my campaign platform – protecting jobs."

"Well, we're going to help Mark Tidemore protect *his* job as mayor," declared Ben Bentley. "And I'm going to donate $50,000 to his reelection campaign."

"What campaign?" said Ken Wurgler. "Mark only puts up a few yard signs around town."

Ben shook his head. "That was back when he had no competition."

"What's Ken here going to do that would even be considered competition?" laughed Edgar Ridenour.

Wurgler straightened his toupee. "Lots," he said, pounding on the table to make his point. "I'm going to call for a public debate. Let's see how Mayor Tidemore defends his public record. I'm going straight for the jugular."

CHAPTER SEVEN

Murder, He Wrote

Barffy's death was topic of the day. The Town Council was busy doing damage control. The Crazy Carnival had been closed down the moment Barffy dropped dead. With a whole week to go, the event was a financial disaster for Caruthers Corners. Good fodder for Ken Wurgler's campaign.

"That's clown's death was certainly bad luck," sighed Beau Madison. He and Police Chief Jim Purdue were having coffee at Cozy Café, that silver-fronted diner on South Main. It was known for its Never Ending Cup of Coffee. "Good to the Last Drop" as the slogan goes.

"Luck had nothing to do with it," replied Jim Purdue. His cap was on the table, his balding head gleaming under the fluorescents. His expression hinted at things unsaid.

"What are you suggesting?" Beau looked up from his coffee.

"That it wasn't a heart attack."

"What then – a stroke? – a brain aneurism?"

"No, it was murder," said Chief Purdue. "I just can't prove it."

Beau sat down his coffee cup, sloshing a brown puddle onto the Formica tabletop. "What does Doc Medford say?" A quaver in his voice. This was bad news.

"Doc suspects poisoning, but can't find anything. He's sent off for another toxicology analysis. A deeper dive. Maybe it will give us more info."

"Barffy had dinner here at the diner before his act at the Carnival," muttered Maisie as she refilled their coffee mugs. "You don't think he got food poisoning, d'you?"

"No, of course not," said Jim Purdue. But Beau noticed his pal didn't take another sip of his coffee.

"Back to why you think it's murder –"

"Something we haven't released to the public," said the Police Chief. "We found a message in Barffy's dressing room written on the mirror in red greasepaint. It said: TONIGHT IS THE LAST SNIFFING YOU WILL EVER DO, YOU BIG NOSE TRAITOR!"

~ ~ ~

Beau was careful not to repeat Jim Purdue's suspicions to his wife. He knew that would be just the catalyst to get the Quilters Club involved. And Jim didn't need any interference in his investigation. Between the police chief and the coroner, matters were well in hand.

Sure, Beau's wife and her cronies had successfully solved a number of local crimes. But that wasn't their job. That's why Caruthers Corners had a police department.

Jim had a long history as the town's police chief. He was well respected. And Det. Harry Teague brought a lot of experience to the job. Even Deputy Tommy Truehart could no longer be considered a rookie.

The police didn't need any help from four well-meaning busybodies.

Beau knew the Mayor and the Town Council agreed. Heck, the husbands of all four Quilters Clubbers served on the Town Council.

But his reticence was for naught. Maddy's friend Bootsie had already wormed the story out of her hubby. Phone calls between the women had taken place like a DEFCON 2 alert long before Beau got home from lunch.

~ ~ ~

Bootsie called Maddy. Maddy called Cookie. Cookie called Lizzie. Lizzie called Bootsie. On and on, the calls crisscrossed from house to house with lightning rapidity. That led to a four-way Zoom call. Everybody talking to everybody.

"A threat written on Barffy's mirror the night he died," said Maddy. "That sounds very suspicious."

"Jim thinks it's murder," confirmed Bootsie. "He just can't prove it."

"C'mon, somebody killed that clown," exclaimed Lizzie. "That's as plain as the red nose on his face." She had a tendency toward the dramatic.

"Murder or not, there's a crime here. Penal Code § 422 PC defines the crime commonly known as making criminal threats," recited Cookie, drawing on her trick memory. Highly Superior Autobiographical Memory (HSAM) is a condition that has been identified in fewer than 100 people worldwide. Katherine Ann Bentley (née Johansson) had won the genetic lottery, with a brain as unique as kyawthuite or astatine or osmium.

"Exactly what constitutes a criminal threat?" asked Maddy. Her son-in-law might be a lawyer, but she didn't follow all the finer legal points.

Cookie, of course, had the answer. "'These are threats of death or great bodily injury that are intended to (and that actually do) place victims in reasonable and sustained fear for their safety or the safety of their families.' Therefore, writing that threat on the mirror was a crime."

"Somebody made good on that threat," declared Bootsie. "Murder – that's the real crime here."

"Should the Quilters Club get involved?" asked Maddy. Getting back to the topic at hand.

"Jim would never admit it, but I think he could use some help here," said Bootsie. The chubby housewife thinking of her husband – kinda.

"Then let's do it," said Lizzie.

"Not without an official okay," countered Cookie. "We got in a lot of trouble with our last big case."

"The Cockadoodle?"

"No, the death of that Shakespearean actor."

"True. My hubby was very perturbed over that one," replied Bootsie. "Said we made him look bad."

"Who would we get an okay from?" asked Maddy. "Jim surely won't agree to our getting involved."

"How about your son-in-law?" suggested Cookie, peering over her spectacles. "He's the mayor."

"Mark?"

"Yes, he could give us his blessing. Then Jim couldn't complain," nodded Bootsie. "After all, Mark is his boss."

"Well –" said Maddy.

And that's how the Quilters Club got involved.

CHAPTER EIGHT

Small Town Politics

On Tuesday morning, Mark the Shark called a meeting with his closest advisors. Now that Ken Wurgler had announced his candidacy for mayor, a strategy session was in order.

"Damn fool doesn't have a chance," observed Edgar Ridenour. "But he's determined to stir up some dust." The former bank president was a good judge of people. He knew Wurgler was a man of weak character despite his high ambitions.

"Let him," said Beau Madison. "Everybody knows Ken is all talk and no action. Mark's record speaks for itself."

"We'll still need to respond to his allegations. That you have somehow put jobs at risk. We'll need to mount a campaign of sorts," said Ben Bentley. "I've pledged a war chest of $50,000."

"That much?" responded Mark. "We usually only spend a few thou on yard signs, a billboard or two."

"Forget that. This year we're going all out. We're going to drive over ol' Ken with a bulldozer," declared Ben. He was a short, powerful man, a former high school wrestling champ. Everything he did had an aura of aggression, despite his inwardly gentle nature. He'd been the one to donate land to establish the retreat for retired circus animals – Haney Bros.

Zoo and Exotic Animals Refuge. And he was a pack leader with the Sons of Anthony Wayne, the camper organization. He was good with boys, exhibited in his relationship with his adopted son Gus.

"What do you have in mind?" asked Mark Tidemore. Growing a little nervous. He knew his friends meant well, but sometimes they got carried away.

"In addition to yard signs and billboards, we'll buy some radio and TV advertising, maybe a full-page ad in the *Burpyville Gazette*. Maybe some sky writing," said Ben, eyes dancing with enthusiasm.

Edgar was getting into the swing of it. "How about we hold a rally?" he suggested. "Rent a food truck that serves free hot dogs. Root beer for everyone."

"What if we got a celebrity endorsement?" offered Chief Purdue.

"Like who?"

"Maybe Missy Montana. She's a hometown girl. Doesn't she have a new movie coming out? Or Hitch Richardson. Isn't he an old college buddy of yours, Mark?"

"I guess we could do that," acquiesced Mark Tidemore. "But do you really think it's necessary? I'd rather be judged on my own merits."

"Let's not pull any punches," encouraged Ben. "We've gotta hit Ken Wurgler with everything we've got. If he somehow got elected, it would be disastrous for the town. Everything would come to a screeching halt."

"Ken's an ineffectual dolt," Edgar agreed. "And that's being generous."

"True," said Beau. "Ken Wurgler couldn't find his own butt with two hands and a flashlight."

~ ~ ~

"Where is it?" squealed Sissy Jackson. She couldn't find her winning ticket for the Crazy Carnival quilt. It had been right there in her purse. Now, here she stood in the mayor's office, an orderly two-room enclave on the second floor of the Town Hall, ready to redeem her prize, but the little yellow stub was gone!

"You have to have the ticket to claim the quilt," Mark Tidemore gently reminded the girl. He'd just returned to his office from the political strategy session and was running late for lunch. He had promised to meet his mother-in-law. And you didn't keep Maddy Madison waiting.

"I had it right here." She turned her purse upside down, emptying the contents on his desk. Comb, mirror, chewing gum, rubber bands, hairpins, even a tube of lipstick (don't tell her grandfather). But no ticket.

"Maybe you left it at home," he said, glancing at his watch. "Come back with it this afternoon and you can pick up the quilt."

"My ticket was here in the change pocket of my purse. And now it's gone!"

"Don't worry, you will find it, hon."

"What if somebody stole it?"

"It wouldn't do them any good. We will know if somebody else tries to claim the prize."

"Honest, I had the winning number. 756F9K – see, I memorized it."

The mayor gave her an encouraging smile. "I believe you, Sissy. But you have to turn in the ticket to win. That's the rule."

CHAPTER NINE

Maddy's Summit Meeting

Maddy was waiting in her usual booth when Mark Tidemore came pushing through the revolving door at Cozy Café. "Sorry I'm late," he apologized, sliding into the red leatherette seat. "Sissy Jackson it seems won the Crazy Carnival quilt, but lost the ticket."

"She had it this morning. I saw it."

"Should we bend the rules and give her the quilt without the ticket?"

"No, she will find it," Maddy chuckled. "That girl would lose her head if it wasn't fastened on."

"She may be forgetful, but she can certainly sing. Her performance of 'My Favorite Things' in *The Sound of Music* was a showstopper."

"Sissy is quite the little entertainer."

"She's sure to be chosen Most Talented in her high school class," he nodded. "At least, that's Aggie's prediction."

"I agree," said Maddy. Then she abruptly changed the subject. "Rumor is, you have some competition in this year's mayoral race."

Mark raised his eyebrows with dismay. "Ken Wurgler? I'd hardly call him competition."

"Still –"

"My team had a meeting this morning. Ben is putting up money for some campaign promotions. We're not taking Ken for granted. He says he has N.L. Purdue's backing."

"And you have his brother Bobby Ray's endorsement. As well as mine."

"Mine too," affirmed Maisie Walters as she delivered two cups of coffee. She considered herself a part of every conversation that took place in Cozy Café.

Maddy and her sister bumped fists as a sign of solidarity. You wouldn't know it at first glance, but being heirs to the Hoople fortune, Maddy and Maisie controlled more wealth than N.L. and Bobby Ray put together.

"Thanks. But you didn't invite me to lunch to talk about my reelection. What's on your mind?"

"Barffy the Red-Nosed Clown."

~ ~ ~

Sissy turned her purse inside out. No ticket. But she'd had it just this morning; showed it to Mrs. Madison while she had breakfast at the big Victorian house on Melon Pickers Row. How could she have lost it between there and the Town Hall?

She thought back, retracing her steps in her mind: After noshing on watermelon pancakes, she'd headed up the steep hill to the Perricock Museum of Science and History. One wing was a science museum, another the historical society, and the third serving as the town's new library. She had turned in an overdue book – paying the late fee of 5¢ – before making her way to the mayor's office to claim the Crazy Carnival quilt she'd won.

Had she dropped the ticket on the way?

No, it had been safely tucked inside her purse. Only time she'd opened it was to extract the nickel late fee. Maybe she'd dropped the ticket then? Could it be laying there on the library's front desk?

If so, she'd be all right. Dorothy Starcatcher, the head librarian, would have found it on the counter and saved it for her. The woman was thoughtful like that.

Sissy breathed a sigh of relief.

CHAPTER TEN

Asking Permission ... kinda

"What do you want to know about Barffy the Red-Nosed Clown?" asked Mark Tidemore cautiously. He knew his mother-in-law well enough to be suspicious when she ambushed him with an out-of-the-blue topic.

"Word is, he was murdered."

"Who says?"

"Jim told Bootsie. You know he can't keep anything from her."

"Well, there *was* a message written on Barffy's dressing room mirror that makes one question the clown's death," he admitted.

"The Quilters Club would like to help out, but we'd prefer to be invited."

"That's never going to happen. You'd be stepping on Chief Purdue's toes."

"He's the one who spilled the beans to his wife. Can't blame us for stepping up like good citizens."

"C'mon, Maddy. I don't need any trouble when I'm running for re-election."

"You said Ken was no competition."

"Appearances. I can't be showing favoritism to my mother-in-law."

"Nobody will know we're looking around. We will be very discrete."

He smiled. "Like an elephant tiptoeing down squeaky steps."

"Cute. But you know I can't hold the girls back. They are very headstrong."

"That's for certain. Let me think. Maybe there's a way to disguise your snooping."

"Snooping? Don't you mean investigating?"

"Whatever. But let's make sure it's *sub rosa*."

"You mean undercover?"

"Not exactly. What if I appointed you gals to head up a fact-finding committee to determine when we should reschedule the carnival. That way you could poke about without it being too obvious."

"Wouldn't you normally ask Gimble & Gimble to do something like that?"

"We will. But in the meantime you can pretend like that's your assignment. I'll even make sure there's a squib about the appointment of the committee in the *Gazette*."

"Deal. We might even come up with some good ideas for the next carnival while we're at it."

"Don't get carried away. There are some strings attached."

"No problem," Maddy smiled demurely. "What?"

So he told her.

Maddy shrugged. "Let's order lunch," she said, picking up a menu. "I have a Quilters Club meeting this afternoon."

CHAPTER ELEVEN

Crazy Quilts

Tuesday afternoons marked the weekly gatherings of the Quilters Club. These days they met in the crafts area at the Hoople Quilting Heritage Museum, a large squarish room piled high with fabric samples and quilt blocks and assorted textile scraps. A worktable took up the center of the room, flanked by cushioned seats that were comfortable for sewing.

Having finished the Pictorial Quilt for the Caruthers Corners Crazy Carnival's auction, they now were working on Crazy Quilts, a good way to use up stray fabric scraps.

A Crazy Quilt looks like stitched-together confetti, the colors dazzling, each fabric piece differing from the other – a crazy array of silk, satin, and other materials, sometimes embellished with extensive embroidery, ribbons, needlepoint, and hand-painted blocks.

"Early quilts made in the crazy style were often more for show than practical usage," pointed out Lizzie Ridenour. As Director of the Hoople Quilting Heritage Museum, she liked to lecture her friends on the subject. "They sometimes took the form of small 'lap robes,' perfect for decorating the parlor."

"In Colonial times, quilts were objects of the wealthy because threads, needles, and cotton could be very expensive," Cookie chimed in, repeating something she'd come across on the Internet. Her eidetic memory allowed her to cite anything she'd ever read. Facts stuck like glue. "Only after 1793, when Eli Whitney revolutionized the textile industry by inventing the cotton gin, were quilts economical to produce."

"That's right," Lizzie took back the conversation. "In the Victorian period – the late 1880s until 1900 – Crazy Quilts became quite fashionable. Victorian-era women embellished the embellished. They stitched most pieces using pure silk or cotton twist, some with a single strand of embroidery thread. Today, collectors will pay between $2,000 and $5,000 for a period Crazy Quilt in good condition."

"All we have to do is wait a hundred years for our Crazy Quilts to become valuable," joked Bootsie.

"Maybe a little longer for yours," retorted Lizzie. Her friend was the least skilled among them at the art of sewing.

"C'mon, my stitches are improving," the tubby woman with the pixie hairstyle protested petulantly.

"Well, some better," Lizzie conceded.

Maddy passed around some watermelon cupcakes she'd baked that morning. They took turns providing snacks each week. Pies, cakes cookies, scones.

"Any news on the death of that clown?" asked Lizzie. She was a sucker for gossip.

"Jim still thinks it's murder," offered Bootsie. She was the Quilters Club's pipeline into the police department.

"Are we going to investigate?" asked Cookie.

Maddy offered a wicked smile "Do Pooh bears picnic in the woods?" she replied to her friend's question.

"Did Mark gave us the go-ahead?"

"Yes," nodded Maddy. "He says he will appoint us to a planning committee for the next carnival. That will allow us to poke around without embarrassing the police department."

"What does he want in return?" asked Bootsie. She knew getting his permission would come with a price.

"He wants us to retire after this one."

"Will we?" asked Cookie.

"We'll see," said Maddy with a shrug. "Depends how this one goes."

~ ~ ~

Sissy stood at the library's front desk, tears staining her brown cheeks. "It's got to be here," she sniffled. "There's no place else I could have lost it."

Dorothy Starcatcher shook her head, blonde hair swaying with the gesture. Her spectacles made her eyes appear owl-like. "Sorry, dear. If I had seen a ticket, I would have put it in the Lost and Found drawer, along with all the eyeglasses, lipsticks, and keys. No tickets here, I'm afraid." She waved her hand at the open drawer as if settling the subject.

"I so wanted that big quilt. I've got just the place to hang it in my bedroom."

"I will keep my eyes open," the librarian assured her. "Maybe it will turn up."

Dorothy Starcatcher's fanciful last name came from her mother's stage persona. Her mom had been a magician's assistant for The Great Wizardini. The retired illusionist and his sister lived in the big monolith on the adjacent hill in the Hoople Senior Living Home. It used to be the residence of the eccentric Hoople sisters, as well as Maddy and her family.

The Great Wizardini – Ernst Hegler by name – was one of the more famous people in Caruthers Corners. He had enjoyed a long career, appearing on stages across the Midwest – and once even on *The Ed Sullivan Show*.

In his honor, a back corner of the library housed the Great Wizardini Magic Room, a place for mothers to park their children while browsing the bookshelves. One day a week Ernst Hegler came in to teach kids magic tricks.

Sissy took a seat on a nearby wooden bench, pausing to rethink her morning's travels. Was there someplace else she might have lost that ticket? No, nothing came to mind.

Sitting there near the Magic Room made her think of The Great Wizardini's sleight-of-hand performances – palming cards, making coins disappear, picking pockets. Hmm, could someone have picked her pocket ... well, picked her purse to be more accurate?

Maybe.

But who?

CHAPTER TWELVE

Doc Medford

Dr. Franklin Delano Medford's medical practice was located next door to Yost & Yost Funeral Home. This was very convenient for him, considering he also served as the town's part-time coroner. Most of his work was confirming heart attacks. All those fried cheese balls and pork tenderloin cutlets that Hoosiers loved to eat came with a price.

However, Doc Medford's autopsy of Walter Ambrose Bradford showed no indication of a massive pulmonary embolism or myocardial infarction. No heart problems at all.

Doc's report read:

> The body was of a man 72 years of age. To external appearance, he was quite normal. Opening the chest, the heart and lungs appear normal. I slit open the pulmonary artery and its major branches. There were no emboli in them. I opened the pericardium and found the heart normal in appearance. I detached the heart and placing it on a table slit open each the arteries that supplied the muscles of the heart. There were no clots. The inner surfaces of the heart's blood vessels were in perfect

condition. The rest of the body was normal.
Cause of death: undetermined.

That notwithstanding, he would change it to heart attack. Just to keep things tidy.

He suspected poison, but he had no proof.

Doc relied on the State Police labs for tox reports. Their first pass on Walt Bradford's death showed nothing. No poisons found in the stomach contents. No toxins in the blood stream. No Mees' Lines on the fingernails. No smell of bitter almonds or garlic or freshly mowed hay. No rashes or abnormal skin coloring. So now they were doing a second run, looking for more exotic poisons, ones not covered in a typical analysis.

They already had ruled out arsenic, cyanide, strychnine. Maybe it was something unusual, like curare, ricin, thallium, or botulism.

Doc hated tricky cases.

~ ~ ~

A rugged-looking man with a square chin and broad shoulders, Det. Harry Teague was the police department's lead investigator. He looked the part of a cop you might see on *Law & Order*. Today, he was working with Chief Purdue on the Barffy the Clown case. His assignment was to find the clown who had left a threatening message on Barffy's mirror. The theory being that the person who left that message was the murderer ...

Yes, like the Chief, Harry was convinced it was murder. He'd been a cop too long to believe in coincidences. He considered it highly unlikely that Barffy would immediately drop dead after receiving a death threat.

But so far they couldn't even pinpoint the cause of the clown's demise. No gunshot wounds, no puncture marks, no strangulation abrasions, no bruises or lacerations. It had to be poison. But the first tox report was negative.

Another problem, the only witness to someone writing that message on the mirror was Birdie Longstreet, a most unreliable witness. The old woman said it was written by another clown.

If she were correct, that should narrow down the number of suspects. According to records, there had been 14 clowns at the carnival: Barffy, Sparkplug, and the 12 goofballs in the Klown Kar Krew.

Barffy was dead. Sparkplug was none other than the local fire chief. So the clown who left the message had to be one of the clown car clowns.

Guess he'd be making a trip to Chicago. That's where the 12 came from. A quick, last-minute booking through a Windy City agency called Littleton & Co.

CHAPTER THIRTEEN

Birdie Longstreet

Being low man on the totem pole, Deputy Tommy Truehart had been assigned to investigate Birdie Longstreet's complaint about being threatened by a clown. He knew it was going to be a waste of time. Nobody took Birdie's report seriously. Last week she had claimed she'd seen an African lion in her backyard. It turned out to be Alexander the Great, Maisie's part-time tomcat.

The deputy dutifully made notes as Birdie repeated her story about walking into a wrong door at the carnival and coming upon a green-haired clown scrawling a message on the mirror. As she recalled the words, it was something about sniffing flowers. Or smelling the roses. Or something like that.

"And he threatened you?"

"Yes, absolutely. I would have hit him with my umbrella – I thought it might rain, so I brought it with me to the carnival – but he had an accomplice with him. I was afraid they would overpower me. Y'know, to have their sordid way with me."

"Wait – you're saying there were *two* clowns?"

"Yes indeed. One writing on the mirror; the other lurking at the other door."

"If one of the clowns had green hair, what did the other look like?"

"Hard to tell. He was wearing a Halloween monster mask."

~ ~ ~

Randolph Johnson had three eyes, the result of a "vanishing twin" who he called Rex. One of the Crackleton progeny, Three Eyes (as people called him) had been promoted as the main draw at the sideshow for the Caruthers Corners Crazy Carnival. Practically all the Crackleton clan had one disorder or another – the result of years of inbreeding.

In less-politically-correct times, this carnival exhibit would have been called a Freak Show. However, that term's original neutral connotation somehow became negative during the 20th Century. Today, the word *freak* with its literal meaning of "abnormally developed individual" is viewed as pejorative.

Call it what you will, people had been lining up last Friday night to pay 50¢ to view the array of giants and dwarfs and pinheads and lobster boys. People like to gawk at weird folks.

Randolph Johnson didn't mind being put on display. It was for a good cause, bringing visitors to Caruthers Corners. That would help the economy. And provide more people to steal from.

The Crackletons were known for their larceny.

As Randolph liked to joke about his three eyes – "All the better to see you with!" And that Friday night he'd spotted something unusual, a green-haired clown trashing one of the circus dressing rooms. Well, not exactly trashing it, but writing something on the mirror. The message made no sense to him. Something about sniffing with a big nose.

Randolph had been planning on robbing the dressing room. The Freak Show hadn't opened to visitors yet. But when he started to go in, he spotted that stupid clown – talk about a freak! –with all that spikey green hair and carrot-like nose.

At the same time, an old lady had stumbled into the dressing room from the other side, looking confused at first, then frightened when she spied the clown. Her level of terror went up a notch or two when the bozo turned to her and threatened to slit her throat. What happened next was unknown to Randolph, for he turned and ran. He and his parasitic twin Rex only had one neck between them, and he had no intention of offering it to a deranged harlequin for razor practice.

He wondered if the old lady had survived. But the *Burpyville Gazette* reported no murders, only the heart attack of someone called Barffy.

CHAPTER FOURTEEN

Col. Oscar Owensby

Walter Bradford's medical records showed no history of heart problems. Still myocardial infractions could be sudden and surprising.

His manager – an old circus pro known as Col. Oscar Owensby – confirmed that Bradford had not shown any of the traditional risk factors. No high blood pressure; never smoked; no sign of diabetes; got plenty of exercise; cholesterol was relatively low.

"There goes my meal ticket," Col. Owensby groused about the clown's death. "Barffy was my very last client. I've been at this for over half a century. Not many of us old-timers left."

Chief Jim Purdue pressed: "Any enemies? Anybody who might wish him harm?"

"Naw. He was a clown, f' gosh sakes."

"Aren't some people afraid of clowns?"

"Sure. There's a name for it – coulrophobia. But most folks find them funny."

~ ~ ~

Bootsie repeated her hubby's conversation with Col. Oscar Owensby.

"Coulrophobia," said Cookie, drawing on her photographic memory. "There was a recent study. More than fifty percent of the respondents said they were scared of clowns at least to some degree, with 5% saying they were 'extremely afraid' of them. Interestingly, this percentage was slightly higher than reported for other phobias, such as fear of animals, heights, closed spaces, and flying."

"Thank you, Miss Know-It-All," teased Lizzie. Her friend's trick memory always astounded her.

Cookie took this as encouragement to continue. "The study also found that women are more afraid of clowns than men. The reason is not clear, but it mirrors the findings on other phobias such as the fear of snakes and fear of spiders."

"We women are delicate creatures," posited Lizzie, fluffing her red coiffure.

"Snakes don't scare me," said Bootsie. "But keep spiders away."

"I used to be afraid of Ronald MacDonald," Maddy admitted. "Those big clodhopper feet and unruly red hair, he looked like a homicidal maniac to me."

~ ~ ~

"Barffy the Red-Nosed Clown kinda scared me," admitted Jason Jonathan Floyd, patriarch of the Flying Floyds. "We played some of the same venues. But I kept my distance. So did my kids."

The aerialist was having a sugar cream pie at Cozy Café while giving an interview to Lucius Plancus, a reporter with WZUR. A 300-pound redhead, Plancus was derisively known to his coworkers as The Jolly Red Giant.

"Scared you in what way?" pressed the oversized newsman.

"He had a temper. Could go from friendly to confrontational in a split second. And with that white facepaint, you couldn't see it coming."

"He reminded me of Pennywise, that killer clown in those *It* movies," interjected Priscilla, Floyd's daughter. Prissy had followed in her daddy's footsteps ... er, on his trapeze bar to be more precise. These days, the pretty twentysomething was the star of the show, known for her ability to spin upside down, then execute a double backward upside-down flip into the net. Not many aerialists could do that.

"Those movies are based on a Stephen King novel," Plancus nodded. "I'm a big fan."

"Barffy did look a bit like Pennywise, except for that big red nose," agreed Jason Jonathan Floyd. "That nose was Barffy's trademark. He'd walk along the edge of the ring, sniffing at people in the audience, then magically extract things – balloons, rubber chickens, you name it – from each of them. He was as much a slight-of-hand expert as he was a clown."

"A clown that works among the audience is known as a Carpet Clown," explained Prissy. "His act was mostly based on walkarounds."

"Walkarounds?"

"That's when a clown strolls around the ring performing visual gags that can easily be done again for another section of the audience."

"He has a lot of interaction with the audience," nodded her father.

"Did you ever have a run-in with him?"

"Naw. We Floyds are a tightknit clan. We kept our distance from him."

Plancus moved his microphone closer. "But you said he had a temper. Did you see it in action?"

58

"More than once."

"So who did he have confrontations with? Anybody who might have wanted to see him dead?"

Jason Jonathan Floyd frowned. "I thought they said he died from a heart attack."

"The verdict's still out on that. Can you give me any names of people who disliked him?"

The aerialist snorted. "About anyone who ever met him. He was a most disagreeable fellow."

"Try William Tuckman," said Priscilla.

"Who's that?" asked Lucius Plancus.

"Another clown. Billy Tuckman is a Clown Boss; he drives the clown car. They got into a tussle during rehearsals."

"Over what?"

"Who knows?" she shrugged. "Professional rivalry, I assume."

CHAPTER FIFTEEN

Littleton & Co.

Following a tip from Lucius Plancus, Det. Harry Teague drove his cruiser up to Chicago to interview William Tuckman. With the closing of the Crazy Carnival, the 12 members of the Klown Kar Krew had returned to Chi-Town. They worked the entire Midwest, but this was their home base. Harry had planned on checking out all the clowns, but the WZUR reporter gave him someone specific to focus on. Hopefully, that would save a lot of time.

Harry met Tuckman at his booker's office. The lettering on the rippled-glass door proclaimed: WORLD'S GREATEST LIVE ACTS. Beneath that, it stated LITTLETON & CO.

Eric J. Littleton ushered the detective into a small conference room where Billy Tuckman was waiting, eyes dancing crazily, a nervous tic like something you'd find on the face of an Arkham Asylum inmate. Billy wasn't wearing any greasepaint or costume, so he looked like your run-of-the-mill lunatic.

"Thanks for meeting with me, Mr. Tuckman. I'd like to ask you a few questions about Walter Bradford."

"Barffy?"

"Yes, the clown who died last Friday night at the opening of Caruthers Corners Crazy Carnival. You were on the program that night, right?"

"Yes, my troupe was there, but we never performed. Everything shut down after Barffy dropped dead. Just like him to screw everything up."

"You didn't like him?"

"Nobody liked him. He was a jerk."

"Now, now, let's not talk ill of the dead," interjected Littleton. He offered a weak, unconvincing smile. His bowtie did not give him a serious air. Maybe working with clowns had rubbed off on him.

"It's true," insisted Billy Tuckman. "Ask anybody."

Harry Teague looked down at his notes. "You drive the clown car?"

"Right. A modified Fiat 500. Holds twelve if we pack 'em in right. They fit like a jigsaw puzzle."

"Modified?"

"We remove the seats, extend the trunk space. Making as much room as we can. It's not easy to get a dozen people into an itty-bitty Italian sub-compact car."

"There's twelve of you in all?"

"That's right – counting me as the driver."

"Have you guys played other gigs with Barffy the Red-Nosed Clown?"

Tuckman nodded, his facial tics like Mexican jumping beans under the skin. "Sure, lotsa times. We were second banana to him at Ringling before it closed down."

"Somebody said there might have been some professional jealousy between the acts," stated the detective, looking down at his notes.

"There's professional jealousy between *all* acts," replied Billy Tuckman. "That's the nature of show biz."

"That's true," offered Eric Littleton. "I've been in this business forty-two years. I oughta know. All my clients hate each other."

"Was Barffy your client too?"

"Sure was. My biggest moneymaker. Gonna be a big loss for me. He was gonna headline for Ringling when they reopen next year."

"We can handle that spot," volunteered Tuckman. "My Klown Kar Krew is always a hit."

Littleton looked dubious. "That will be up to the folks at Ringling. I'm sure it will either be you guys or Topsy."

"Topsy?" repeated Harry Teague.

"Topsy the Green Goblin. He's a scary clown. The audience loves the way he spooks them. Strutting around the ring snarling at them."

"Does he have green hair?"

"Sure does," nodded the booker.

"Big deal," said Billy Tuckman. "So do I. My clown's called Sweet Pea."

CHAPTER SIXTEEN

The Clown Car

The origin of the clown car is credited to a German-born clown named Lou Jacobs (né Johann Ludwig Jacob). As noted, clown cars are tiny vehicles into which clowns squeeze themselves "for a few cheap laughs."

On average, each clown takes up three cubic feet, so mathematically speaking, about 40 clowns would be able to fit inside a car with 120 cubic feet. However, during a show, only about 12 to 21 clowns would typically fit into the car.

In addition to the midget clown car, Lou Jacob's act included performing as a one-man band, where he attached several instruments to his body and played a raucous tune by moving his limbs. Jacobs managed to play the harmonica while keeping the bass drum, cymbals and bells going.

Jacobs appeared with Ringling Bros. and Barnum & Bailey Circus for more than 60 years. Along with Emmett Kelly, he was featured in Cecil B. DeMille's movie, *The Greatest Show on Earth*. Jacobs was inducted into the International Clown Hall of Fame in 1989.

~ ~ ~

"What about the other members of your clown car troupe – any of them have green hair?" asked Det. Harry Teague.

Billy Tuckman screwed up his face to think. "Hm, just Gary."

"Who?"

"Gary Griffin. He's known as Green Grasshopper. Because he's so lean and limber. At 6-foot-4, the tallest member of the Krazy Kar Krew. He has to form the letter M to fit inside the car. The little guys – we have three midgets in the group – tuck themselves into the angles of his body."

"Maybe I should talk with, uh, Green Grasshopper too," said the detective.

"What's this obsession with green-haired clowns?" asked Eric Littleton. Protective of his clients.

"A witness spotted a clown with green hair in Barffy's dressing room. We want to talk with him."

"Wasn't me," Billy Tuckman held up his hand, palms like stop signs. "Couldn't have been Gary either. All the clown car clowns stay together before a performance, getting in the zone."

"Zone?"

"Takes the proper mental attitude to squeeze yourself into a tangle of a dozen guys inside a tiny metal cube. Does tend to be claustrophobic."

"So the other ten can vouch for you and this Gary?"

"Right as rain. Neither of us could have been the clown your witness saw."

"What about this Topsy?"

Eric Littleton spoke up. "Topsy – Kyle Brownell, that is – wasn't booked for the Caruthers Corners Crazy Carnival."

"What other clowns were?"

"None. Oh, wait – there was that one called Sparkplug. I believe he's your town fire chief, right?"

~ ~ ~

For years now, Freddie Madison had assumed the persona of Sparkplug the Fire Prevention Clown as a side gig, performing at children's parties and more recently on weekends at the Haney Bros. Zoo & Exotic Animal Refuge.

The greasepaint was a way of hiding his badly burned face. His body was a roadmap of scars acquired when he was working with Fire-Rescue in Atlanta. Caught in an apartment building conflagration, he had been burned on 30% of his body. His survival had been iffy, fifty-fifty at best.

Slowly but surely, he was coming to terms with his gnarled Gremlin-esque looks. Longtime friends no longer seemed to notice his deformed countenance. Sometimes he forgot about it too.

The main point for Det. Harry Teague was that Sparkplug the Clown did not have green hair. His hairless pate – actually a skull cap – was as smooth as an egg. That crossed him off the list. Not that Harry expected the town's fire chief to be threatening little old ladies. Or writing off-putting messages on mirrors.

CHAPTER SEVENTEEN

The Juggling Juggernauts

Making sure he covered all the bases, Det. Teague decided to interview the Juggling Juggernauts, that trio of unicyclists who had been on the Crazy Carnival program with Barffy.

Larry, Moe, and Spike Calabash – the Juggling Juggernauts – were also clients of Littleton & Co., so Harry Teague could easily check them out while he was here in Chicago. Besides, that gave him an excuse to stay over. He wanted to catch a Second City performance while he was in the Windy City. Harry was a big fan of improvisational comedy. He'd once seen Bill Murray on stage there, back before Saturday Night Live and *Caddyshack*. And he'd caught John Candy one time too.

The three brothers lived in a run-down house on a trash-strewn block on the Southside. They practiced in their garage because it had a smooth cement floor and a high ceiling, perfect for juggling on a one-wheeled cycle.

"Sorry, we can't help you more," said Larry Calabash, the older brother. He seemed to be spokesman for the group. "We were there when Barffy grabbed his throat and keeled over, but we don't know any more than that. Somebody said it was a heart attack."

"We're just trying to be thorough," said the detective, avoiding a direct answer. No need to reveal their suspicions to anyone until Doc Medford's second toxicology report came in. He was betting it would turn up a smoking gun – a hard-to-detect poison like tetrodotoxin or 1080 sodium fluoroacetate.

"The show was canceled the minute Barffy hit the sawdust. We didn't get to perform. Thankfully, we got paid a kill fee – sorry about that expression!"

"Did any of you leave ringside before the show started?"

"Naw, we were riding around in circles, practicing. We warm up that way before every performance."

"Did you see any of the other acts leave the tent?"

"Not me," said Spike.

"Me neither," echoed Moe. "You have to concentrate when you're juggling bowling pins. They can leave a knot if you let one hit you."

"Yeah, I got a concussion one time," Spike nodded. "Let my concentration go down. That hurt."

"I saw the Flying Floyds wandering around," said Larry. "I wasn't paying as much attention I should've been getting ready for the act. But it was just a nothing gig in a Podunk town ... no offense."

"Anything else?"

"Might have seen Sweet Pea disappear for a few minutes, but I'm not sure." Larry shrugged. "What's it matter?"

"Just asking," said Det. Teague, scribbling in his notebook. Sweet Pea was accounted for, alibied by his clown car comrades.

~ ~ ~

For any of you who don't know, a unicycle is a one-wheeled bicycle – that is, a vehicle that touches the ground with only one wheel. Riding it takes skill and balance.

US patents for a single-wheeled "velocipede" was granted in 1869 to Frederick Myers and in 1881 to Battista Scuri.

Today's unicycles come in many variations, ranging from the standard Freewheeling version to an ultra-tall chain-driven unicycle known as a Giraffe, from the Ultimate Wheel (a unicycle with no frame or seat, just a wheel and pedals) to a Monocycle (a large wheel inside which the rider sits as in a hamster wheel).

Most riders use the smooth Freewheeling Style, but clowns and other circus performers often employ a Comedy Style, one that exaggerates the perceived difficulty of riding a unicycle to create a comedic effect.

Notable unicyclists include American clown Skeeter Reece, German jugglers Rudy Horn and Ernest Montego, Chinese acrobat Jiang Yan Jing, and the late Michael Nesmith of The Monkees.

Larry, Moe, and Spike Calabash were up-and-comers in the circus world, the newest clients signed by Littleton & Co. He had hopes for them. Clowns on unicycles always played well.

CHAPTER EIGHTEEN

The History of Clowns

The first record of clowns can be traced back to the Fifth Dynasty of Egypt, around 2400 BC. Pharaohs used to keep African Pygmies in the Royal Courts to amuse their families. Clowns also served a socio-religious role, with priests sometimes playing the clown role as well. It was thought they brought good health to those who watched them perform.

Traditionally, the clowns of ancient Greece were bald and wore padded clothes to appear larger. Strolling clowns were seen in Sparta as early as the 7th Century B.C. Known as *deikeliktas* (or "those who put on plays"), these clowns portrayed everyone from soldiers to fools, witches and slaves to Greek gods.

Roman clowns often wore pointed hats and were the butts of the jokes. They fell into four categories: Sannio (maskless mimes); Stupidus (who gave us the word *stupid*); Scurra (where we get the word *scurrilous*); and Moriones (who led to the word *moron*).

During the Medieval era, a court jester or fool was sometimes a member of a nobleman's household, his role being to entertain the master's guests.

Originating with Italy's *commedia dell'arte*, the Harlequin appeared in England early in the 17th Century. He was typically masked and dressed in a diamond-patterned costume. The Harlequin was routinely paired with a clown as his foil.

Joseph Grimaldi invented the modern clown in 1801. With his face covered in white makeup, mouth painted with an exaggerated grin, he set the standard. Even today, British clowns are called "Joeys" after him.

The modern circus can be traced back to 1768 with the opening of Philip Astley's London Riding School. Astley added a clown to his shows to amuse the spectators between equestrian sequences.

An Englishman named John Bill Ricketts brought the circus to the United States in 1792.

In 1825, Joshuah Purdy Brown was the first circus owner to use a large canvas tent for the circus performance.

Showman P.T. Barnum revolutionized the circus during the 1870s with P.T. Barnum's Grand Traveling Museum, Menagerie, Caravan & Hippodrome, along with the first freak show. This eventually grew into Ringling Bros. and Barnum & Baily Circus – The Greatest Show on Earth.

~ ~ ~

A clown's act is called a "gag." Europeans refer to it as an "entrée." Amateur clowns sometimes refer to it as a "skit" or "sketch."

Gags take place in the ring (a ring gag or production gag), on the track (a track gag or a walkaround), or in the seats. They have a beginning, middle, and end, finishing with a "blow-off."

Gags use many types of blow-offs (endings), but among the most popular are the confetti bucket, the long shirt, a trousers drop, or all clowns exit running – although indoor shows often end a clown gag with a simple blackout.

~ ~ ~

Most historians agree that Matthew Sully was the first American circus clown. Performing with John Bill Ricketts's Circus, the British-born entertainer was adept as a Harlequin, tumbler, and singer.

John Durang was the first circus clown born in America. He performed with Ricketts's circus too.

New Yorker Dan Rice (A/K/A Daniel Mclaren) became the most famous pre-Civil War circus clown. His act included singing, dancing, feats of strength, and trick riding. His trademark was a goat-like Uncle Sam beard.

Emmett Kelly became the preeminent American circus clown with his sad-sack character Weary Willie, based on the hobos of the Great Depression.

Barffy was considered by some as Kelly's hand-picked successor.

CHAPTER NINETEEN

The Fake Colonel

Col. Oscar Owensby was not really a colonel – not even the Kentucky variety. He'd got the idea for the phony title from Elvis Pressley's manager, Col Tom Parker. During the Vietnam War, Oscar had been classified as 4-F. He never served in the military.

Oscar Owensby was a portly man. In his wide-bodied seersucker suit, he looked out-of-balance, like he might fall over without that ivory-handled cane to prop him up like a tripod. He liked rich food, beer, and cigars – in that order.

His client list had dwindled over the years, but past clients had included Bombo the Human Cannonball, Jacko the Three-Armed Juggler, R&B singer Millicent Marbles, and a lion tamer who had been eaten by his big cats. No, not Siegfried or Roy – but his guy had played Las Vegas once or twice.

Finally, the Colonel was down to Barffy the Red-Nosed Clown. Still a Ringling headliner, Barffy kept food on the table, beer in the fridge, and cigars in the humidor.

Owensby lived year-round in Sarasota near the old circus grounds, his house an elaborate affair well beyond his means. Debt was piling up. And recently, Barffy had been talking of retiring. That wouldn't do.

After booking Barffy for that two-bit Indiana carnival, there was nothing on the schedule till Ringling reopened. That was only a few months away. The Colonel could hold out till then. He'd taken a second mortgage on his house. It had been designed by F. Burrall Hoffman, one of the famed Florida architect's later works.

When this talk of retiring came up again, Owensby had flown up to the Hoosier State to talk to his client. At 72, Barffy had a few more good years in him.

The Colonel simply needed to explain it to him in the right way.

~ ~ ~

Col. Owensby settled in at Hotel Sieur de LaSalle on the east side of Burpyville. It was a holdover from the Gilded Age, that era extending roughly from 1877 to 1896, a pejorative term for that time of materialistic excesses combined with extreme poverty. The term came from one of Mark Twain's lesser-known novels, *The Gilded Age: A Tale of Today* (1873).

Named after French explorer Rene-Robert Cavelier, the hotel was built in the châteauesque style. As designed by Henry Ives Cobb, it features a heavily ornamented façade flanked by elaborate towers and spires, with a steeply-pitched roof. The hotel advertises 65 luxury rooms and suites and a "Pere Marquette" fine dining restaurant.

Col. Owensby liked to travel in style. Fortunately, the town of Caruthers Corners was paying for his and Walt's accommodations. Their rooms were two doors apart. That was convenient, in that the Colonel had some serious matters to discuss with his client.

You might say this conversation was a matter of life and death.

~ ~ ~

Beau Madison stepped up behind his wife's chair, leaned forward to massage her shoulders. They felt tense, but a few minutes with his "magic fingers" would take care of that. "So, you wiggled your way in, huh?" he said.

"Whatever are you talking about?"

"Don't try to deny it. I talked to Mark this morning."

"Oh, that."

"Jim is not very happy with you girls."

"He should be. Mark extracted a big price of entry."

"So he said. Do you think you gals can live up to that deal?"

"Of course, Pooh Bear. We're getting a bit long of tooth. Time to hang up our handcuffs."

"You don't have any handcuffs."

"Bet you wish I did," she said sexily.

"Ha! I think I need a safe word."

CHAPTER TWENTY

The Lost Boy

That morning, Mark the Shark met with Bobby Ray Purdue to secure his support in the upcoming mayoral election. You had to massage your major backers.

In addition to being N.L. Purdue's younger brother, Bobby Ray was one of the so-called Lost Boys. He and two friends had disappeared in the Never Ending Swamp back in 1982, but rather than actually being lost they had joined a circus. Returning some thirty years later, Bobby Ray had recovered some rare Grand Watermelon bank notes that had been hidden in his grandmother's patchwork quilt, making him a multimillionaire, even richer than his Fat Cat brother.

They sat in the expansive living room of Bobby Ray's house at the end of Melon Rind Road just off Highway 101. The house was more glass than brick, offering a clear view of his collection of neon jukeboxes, vintage Indian motorcycles, classic Coca-Cola machines, video arcade games, and assorted movie memorabilia. A stuffed Kodiak bear stood near the entrance as if guarding the eccentric collection.

"No need to worry," Bobby Ray assured him. "You've got my backing. You need any campaign funds, just let me know."

"I'm probably good. Ben Bentley put up $50,000."

"I'll match it."

"The election is not far away. I doubt we can spend that much money."

"How many citizens in Caruthers Corners – 3,000?"

"Not quite that many."

"Maybe 2,000 qualified voters?"

"Not that many."

"What say we pay $50 for each vote? Deal done."

Mark made a *tsk*-ing sound. "That would be illegal."

"Picky, picky, picky."

~ ~ ~

"You're sure there were no other clowns at the Crazy Carnival?" pressed Chief Purdue when his detective returned from his trip to Chicago.

"None I can account for."

"Those clown car clowns had alibies?"

"They alibied each other."

"Then I'm stumped," said Jim Purdue. "Who was the clown Birdie saw?"

Harry Teague hesitated. "There could be another answer."

"What's that?"

"Maybe Birdie Longstreet made the whole thing up. She has a long history of making false accusations. She's reported seeing dinosaurs in her backyard, zombies at the funeral home, bank robbers casing the Savings and Loan, even her long-dead husband."

"Could be," agreed the Police Chief. "The woman is definitely batty."

"Both of the green-haired clowns have air-tight alibies."

"But there's still one thing," said Jim Purdue. "*Some*body wrote a note on Barffy's mirror – green-hair or not."

"True."

"Maybe Birdie got the hair color wrong," the Police Chief shrugged.

CHAPTER TWENTY-ONE

Grammy's Undercover Agent

Without ever seeing any DNA evidence, Maisie Walters accepted that she and Maddy Madison were fraternal twins separated at birth. And that they were the secret love children of Herbert Hoople, one of the world-famous quadruplets. And that the quads were in fact fakes, with Herbie being an adopted Crackleton. And the Crackletons being a genetic cesspool.

But she didn't care.

Maisie had no deformities or deficiencies. Her health was good, her mind sound, her life comfortable.

Although she owned Cozy Café, she still helped cook and waitress because she enjoyed it. Everybody knew her; everybody liked her. The food at the silver-fronted diner was good. As the only restaurant in town (ignoring McDonalds and Pizza Hut), it was a goldmine.

Not that Maisie needed the money. As a Hoople heir, she had a trust fund that made Fort Knox seem like a piggy bank. Yet she lived a very modest existence, still ensconced in the little white clapboard house a few streets over from the diner.

Not into crafts or quiltmaking, she had never joined the Quilters Club. Cooking was her thing. However, she supported her sister's sleuthing. It was like a community service.

That's why she acted as what Aggie called "Grammy's undercover agent." Maisie kept her ears open while serving food at the diner, picking up helpful tidbits that she fed back to her sister.

So when Col. Oscar Owensby came in for breakfast, Maisie paid attention, hovering close, refilling his coffee, giving him special attention, chatting him up. He'd been flattered by the attention.

~ ~ ~

Maddy was making watermelon cupcakes when her sister called. Her hands were covered with dough. As it happened, N'yen might be coming home this weekend and he was quite fond of pastry.

The earliest extant description of what is now called a cupcake was in 1796, when a recipe for "a light cake to bake in small cups" was included in *American Cookery* by Amelia Simmons. This watermelon version was Maddy's own recipe.

"Sis, guess who came in this morning?" said Maisie's voice, a bit distance over the phone.

"Bigfoot?"

"No, he goes through the trash out back," she quipped. "But he has to fight Alexander the Great for it."

"Who then?"

"Col. Owensby – that old guy who managed Barffy the Clown."

"So? Did you ask for his autograph?"

"No, I asked him what he was going to do, now that his big client was dead. He said, 'I'm going to retire and count my money.'"

"He's probably packed in the moola, managing big-name performers like Barffy."

"I don't think so. He said Barffy was his last remaining client. That business had been falling off as circuses closed down. I had the impression he was expecting money from some other source."

"What kind of source?"

"Beats me. He said something about Barffy finally paying off big time."

"That's puzzling. Barffy's dead. How can he pay off?""

"Yeah, confused me too. But I thought it might be a clue or something."

"Thanks, Maisie. Col. Owensby being Barffy's manager, I'm sure we will be talking with him. I'll find out what he meant."

CHAPTER TWENTY-TWO

The False Winner

Dorothy Starcatcher stepped up to the mayor's mahogany desk. "Here is the winning ticket," she announced, presenting a yellow stub of cardboard. "756F9K – that's the number listed in the newspaper, right?"

"Well, uh, yes," Mark admitted. "But there must be some mistake."

"Mistake?"

"Another person has claimed to have the winning number for the Carnival quilt."

"Oh, did that person have a ticket?"

"No, but there's reason to believe she lost it."

The blonde woman cocked her head. "Are you suggesting this is not the winning ticket?"

"No, no, nothing like that. Just some mix-up. I'm sure we can clear it up quickly." The Mayor had to be careful how he handled this. Dorothy Starcatcher was a beloved member of the community. In fact, he had hired her as town librarian himself. Wouldn't do to question her veracity. But something was obviously fishy here.

"Should I come back later?"

"That's a good idea. Give me a chance to look into this matter. Come back Monday, if that's okay."

"Of course. I look forward to getting my new quilt."

~ ~ ~

"We've got a problem," said Mark the Shark, not bothering with a hello. He'd phoned Maddy Madison the moment Dorothy Starcatcher left his office.

"What problem? Did Tilly burn your dinner again?"

"It's true your daughter is not the world's best cook, but that's not the issue at hand. Somebody showed up with the winning ticket for the Crazy Carnival quilt."

"But Sissy has the winning ticket —"

"So she says, but we haven't seen it yet."

"I have."

"But she doesn't have it now."

"Obviously she lost it and someone else has found it. Some sneak thief is trying to claim something that's not his."

"Hers, you mean."

"What?"

"The claimant is Dorothy Starcatcher."

"Oh my, that's a problem. We can't accuse the town's librarian of stealing Sissy's ticket."

"Yeah, my thought exactly," said Mark the Shark. "But what *do* we do?"

CHAPTER TWENTY-THREE

Circus Clowns

Simply put, a circus clown is a performer who uses physical humor to entertain audiences at a circus. They often wear colorful clothing, makeup, wigs, and exaggerated footwear. *Clown* comes from the Icelandic word *klunni* which means "a clumsy person."

There are three basic types of circus clowns: the Whiteface, the Auguste and the Character. (Although often recognized separately, the Tramp or Hobo should technically be classified as a Character Clown.)

•The Whiteface Clown is the oldest of the clown archetypes. The Whiteface is traditionally costumed more extravagantly than the other two clown types, often wearing a ruffled collar and pointed hat, a typical "clown suit." The tenor protagonist of Ruggiero Leoncavallo's tragic opera *Pagliacci* usually appears on stage as the Whiteface variety of clown.

•Auguste Clowns are the ones who "get the pies in the face, are squirted with water, are knocked down on their backside, sit accidentally in wet paint, or have their trousers ripped off." Auguste is German slang for "fool." Sometimes called a Red Clown, the basic makeup for an Auguste is red or flesh tone. He is usually costumed in baggy plaids accented with polka dots or loud stripes. Notable examples include Lou Jacobs, Coco the Clown, and Charlie Rivel.

•The Character Clown portrays an eccentric character such as a butcher, a baker, a policeman, a housewife or a hobo. Among these types are Emmett Kelly, Red Skelton, Buster Keaton, and Charlie Chaplin.

Bozo the Clown was an influential Whiteface character. He has been called "The World's Most Famous Clown." TV weatherman Willard Scott played Bozo from 1959 to 1962.

McDonald's mascot, Ronald McDonald, was derived by Willard Scott from the Bozo character. Scott performed as Ronald McDonald in the fast food company's 1963 television spots.

The *Howdy Doody* television show featured a horn-honking Whiteface Clown called Clarabell. Host Buffalo Bob Smith and the Peanut Gallery used to sing this song:

> "Who's the funniest clown we know?
> "Clarabell!
> "Who's the clown on Howdy's show?
> "Clarabell!
> "His feet are big, his tummy's stout,
> "But we could never do without,
> "Clara, Clara, Clarabell!"

Among those who played Clarabell was Bob Keeshan, who later starred on TV as Captain Kangaroo.

One of the most popular clowns on television is Krusty, a character on the animated series *The Simpsons*. A cigarette-smoking cynic with a pacemaker, Herschel Schmoeckel Pinchas Yerucham Krustofsky (supposedly his name) is portrayed as a grumpy individual who often finds himself in predicaments of his own making – such as running up gambling debts to mobsters or cheating on his taxes. Through it all, however, Bart and Lisa Simpson remain Krusty's devoted fans.

~ ~ ~

"A clown's bright red nose is perhaps his most distinguishing feature. Clown noses come in rubber, leather, and foam, each of which has its advantages and disadvantages. The advantages of a foam nose is that it is more breathable than rubber or leather and it can easily mold to whatever size is necessary," explains a website called eHow.

An outlet called the Red Nose Factory invites clown customers to "Pick your nose," a double entendre worth a laugh. Its website explains the process:

> Our noses are all handcrafted. They are sculpted in clay on a plaster face and are than replicated, inside and out, through a series of molds until the final mold, the mother mold, is layered with the highest quality red liquid latex.

The red nose of a clown has been called "the smallest mask in the world." However, this mask is meant to highlight rather than hide. It works like a bull's eye because it brings all the attention right to the middle of the clown's face.

The use of a red nose originated from the ancient Greek theater, where actors would wear masks with exaggerated facial features, including red noses.

The first circus clown to use the red nose is thought to have been Albert Fratellini (1886-1961), applying a prosthetic to symbolize a drunk's red nose.

In the 1920s the red nose was adopted as part of his clown's makeup by Lou Jacobs. "Mr. Jacobs's whiteface makeup with its gargantuan, goofy smile, outlandish eyebrows and the plum-sized nose was the emblem for the Ringling circus," observed *The New York Times*. Jacobs's clown face became an iconic image for Ringling Bros. and Barnum & Bailey's advertising. In 1966, he had the distinction of having his image appear on a U.S. postage stamp.

Barffy had used a bulbous red nose as part of his shtick, to parody his sense of smell. It was a pretty good gimmick.

CHAPTER TWENTY-FOUR

Bad News

Sissy Jackson sat at the island in Maddy's kitchen, wedged on a high stool between Maddy and the mayor. "What's up?" the girl said. "You guys didn't invite me over for watermelon cupcakes."

"Have another one," said Maddy, passing the tray.

"I've had three. May as well tell me what's going on."

"There's a problem with the winning ticket for the Crazy Carnival quilt," said Mark. Getting right to the point.

"What problem? I just have to find it."

"Someone else came up with it," Maddy said, trying to let her down gently.

"That's right," confirmed the mayor.

"How can that be? I had the winning number. Maddy saw it." These days she called Mrs. Madison and her husband by their first names. After all, she was 17 now, nearly grown. And almost a part of the family.

"Yes, I did. But somehow Dorothy Starcatcher has the ticket now. And she has claimed the quilt."

"But that's not fair. How did she get *my* ticket?"

"We don't know," said Mark the Shark. "But I'm going to look into it."

"But my quilt —"

"Dear, we can't be accusing someone like the town's librarian of lying. At least, not without proof. So here's the deal: If you let her claim the quilt, the Quilters Club will sew a very special replacement for you."

"But —"

"And the Quilters Club promises to figure out how Dorothy got her hands on your ticket. There's got to be an interesting explanation."

~ ~ ~

Dorothy Starcatcher phoned her aunt and uncle. "Happy anniversary," she said. "I have a big surprise for you."

"What, pray tell?" asked The Great Wizardini.

"Yes, what?" urged Mary Alice. They had the speaker button on.

"Can't tell you yet. But I'm picking it up Monday. I'll bring it over when I get it."

"We can hardly wait."

"You will love it," Dorothy promised.

"Can't you give us a hint," said The Great Wizardini.

"Ha! You're supposed to be a mind reader," she teased. "Figure it out for yourself."

CHAPTER TWENTY-FIVE

Evil Clowns

Evil clown sightings are more than an urban legend. Because the only evidence of them often being eyewitness reports, they are sometimes called "phantom clowns." But that doesn't mean they're not real.

First reported in 1981 in Brookline, Massachusetts, children said that men dressed up as clowns attempted to lure them into a van. The panic spread, with sightings popping up in Arizona, New Jersey, North Carolina, Brazil, and Honduras. "Menacing" clowns with weapons were reported in Bakersfield, California. And "creepy" clowns were spotted around a cemetery in Chicago.

Serial killer John Wayne Gacy is considered the inspiration for the modern trend of Evil Clowns. In the 1970s, Gacy murdered 33 young men in the Chicago area. When he wasn't killing people, Gacy performed as Pogo the Clown at charity events and children's parties. Despite his claim that "clowns can get away with murder," he was convicted in 1980 and executed by lethal injection in 1994.

Possibly modeled on Gacy, Pennywise the Dancing Clown appears in Stephen King's horror novel *It* (1986). The evil clown was one of the forms that the monstrous It assumed to murder children in fictional Derry, Maine. The subsequent movies were very popular.

The president of the World Clown Association blamed Stephen King for his profession's bad reputation. "The people dressing up are trying to scare people," he said. "No professional clown would ever take part in anything like that."

~ ~ ~

The Internet and social media have given birth to the "stalker clown," people who dress up as clowns and scare people as a prank. Lots of people want to get in on the act.

Take, for instance, Wrinkles the Clown. He was said to be a curmudgeonly homeless man who dressed as a clown and hired himself out to parents to scare misbehaving children. Wrinkles first appeared in a 2015 YouTube video that depicted him emerging from beneath a young girl's bed in the middle of the night. A 2019 documentary titled *Wrinkles the Clown* revealed that this was performance art by a 65-year-old retiree living in Naples, Florida. However, Wrinkles later refuted the character seen in the documentary, saying it was merely a fictional alter ego. The clown's identity remains anonymous to this day.

Doink the Clown was a persona created in 1992 by professional wrestler Matt Osborne for the World Wrestling Federation. The gimmick was that of a sadistic clown who played cruel tricks on fans and other wrestlers to amuse himself and promote his matches.

Martin Evanick was a death metal drummer who enjoyed dressing up as a clown he called Vlad. Convicted of producing child pornography in 2013, he is currently serving a 20-year prison sentence.

In France, a group of clowns began attacking people in 2014. One beat a man with an iron bar; another sliced a victim's hand with an axe; and still another chased schoolchildren with a chainsaw. As a result, the town banned clown costumes.

A major spate of Evil Clown sightings took place in 2016, starting in Wisconsin and South Carolina, then spreading across the US, Canada, and 18 other countries. They were often attributed to mass hysteria or misguided movie promotions. But some of these were caught on video.

"Clown sightings were springing up all over the world. Who were they? What did they want?" one Internet site posed the question. "There were videos of clowns approaching cars in the night, standing in people's gardens, standing perfectly still on the corner of a street in a little country town, holding a balloon."

The Guardian described the craze as "a magic combination of childhood fears, social media, and psychology."

Vox reassured us, "Scary clowns are not coming for your children."

~ ~ ~

Andrew McConnell Stott, Dean of Undergraduate Education at the University of Buffalo, SUNY, has researched these so-called dark clowns. He observes that the idea of "stranger danger" has contributed to people's fear of clowns in general. "The idea of a reckless anarchic clown has mixed in with our fear of strangers around children."

Clowns with their faces hidden behind greasepaint equaled "strangers." A 2008 study found that the vast majority of children view clowns as "frightening and unknowable."

"Clowns deliberately exaggerate the human face and cover the human face with paint so as to make the face less human," says David Wilson, professor of criminology at Birmingham City University. "When a small child is first learning about the world, to have exaggerated features is incredibly disquieting. It makes them question what they are just beginning to feel is normal. Of course, the clown's behavior is meant to be funny, but if you haven't yet developed that sense of the world then you simply view them as odd, scary."

David Kiser, director of talent for Ringling Bros. and Barnum & Bailey Circus, agrees that there has always been a darker edge to clowns. "The characters always reflected society's perversion, with their brand of comedy coming from their appetites for food, drink, and sex, as well as their manic behavior."

In short, clowns *are* scary.

~ ~ ~

Walter Bradford A/K/A Barffy may have been unlikeable, but he wasn't necessarily scary or evil. At least, that's what Col. Owensby said. Bradford had a soft spot, tithed at church, donated to charities, helped old women cross the street. As Barffy's long-time manager, the Colonel ought to know.

But if the green-hair clown encountered by Birdie Longstreet was responsible for Barffy's death, that interloper could indeed be considered an Evil Clown, Chief Jim Purdue told himself.

CHAPTER TWENTY-SIX

Such a Nice Lady

Aggie said, "I can't believe Dorothy Starcatcher would do something like that – steal your winning ticket. She seems like such a nice lady. And her aunt was one of my role models growing up. There's gotta be some mistake."

She and Sissy talked by phone at least once a week. It was a way to keep the friendship intact. And for Aggie to keep up with the happenings back home.

"I couldn't believe it either. But your dad is gonna turn the Crazy Carnival quilt over to her. After all, she has the winning ticket – number 756F9K – in her sneaky little hand. My ticket."

"Have you asked her about it, how she came to have the ticket?"

"No, I don't like to contradict grown white women who hold powerful positions."

"Powerful? She's just a librarian."

"But her aunt works at the Historical Society with Aunt Cookie, her uncle is a world-famous magician, and she reports directly to your daddy."

"Technically, she reports to the Town Council. But I see your point."

"What am I gonna do. I don't want to roll over and play dead."

"You have a habit of doing that," teased Aggie. She was referring to Sissy's irrational reaction to fear by rolling up into a protective ball, a fetal position. A weird psychological quirk that she exhibited from time to time.

"You know I can't help that. Been doing it since I was a tiny child."

"Why don't you go have a private conversation with Dorothy's aunt? Mary Alice Hegler might know what's going on. She's a smart lady."

"I couldn't risk that. Blood is thicker than water. She might tell her niece about my talking with her."

"So what?"

"I'd never be able to check out a library book for the rest of my life – that's what."

"Want me to talk with Dorothy Starcatcher? I'm not afraid to do that. Something stinks here."

"No, I don't want to drag you into this."

Aggie was silent for a moment, obviously thinking. "Hm, maybe we're going about this the wrong way," she said at last. "We know Dorothy Starcatcher stole your ticket. Maybe we should try to figure out *why* she wants that quilt so badly."

~ ~ ~

Aggie's dad had problems of his own. In addition to the financial mess caused by the closure of the Crazy Carnival, he had an upcoming election to manage.

Normally, he didn't put too much effort in the mayoral campaign. The last two times, he had run unopposed. Not that he thought Ken Wurgler would be much competition, but now he at least had to go through the motions.

His self-appointed election committee – Edgar and Ben, with Beau as an advisor – had big plans. With $100,000 pledged by Ben and Bobby Ray, they were going hog-wild – talking about TV ads and sky writing and celebrity endorsements.

Mark Tidemore had vetoed the celebrities and pulled back on the TV spot ads, but they had already hired "Upside Down Lou" to do the sky writing. Faith Ann Ritchie's oldest son, Lou owned the Heads in the Clouds Skydiving School over in Burpyville.

Mark had been more lenient, in that winning the office of mayor was more important now that he'd heard the newly uncovered dirt on Ken Wurgler, that he had been skimming Chamber of Commerce funds. Who would have thought Ken would stoop that low? But the evidence was irrefutable, turned up in an audit by Town Treasurer Percy Palley. If Percy was good at one thing, it was numbers.

Even so, Mark didn't want to use this info in his campaign. Beau and his campaign managers leaned the other way, saying Ken should get his just dessert.

No matter what, the town couldn't have a mayor with his hand in the till.

CHAPTER TWENTY-SEVEN

The Second Tox Report

The second toxicology analysis came back as ricin. Doc Medford wasn't surprised. He had expected something exotic like that.

Ricin is a highly potent poison produced from the seeds of the castor oil plant (*Ricinus communis*). A carbohydrate-binding protein, ricin can be deadly when inhaled, ingested, or injected. As few as five to ten micrograms per kilogram can be lethal.

No known antidote exists for ricin.

Accidental exposure to ricin was highly unlikely. It would take a deliberate act to use it as a poison. That made Walter Bradford's death a homicide. Doc would be amending the official Death Certificate to Homicide.

People can be poisoned by breathing in ricin mist or powder. If inhaled, ricin can cause respiratory failure. If swallowed, it can shut down the liver and other organs, resulting in death. The amount of ricin that can fit on the head of a pin is said to be enough to kill an adult if properly prepared.

There is no clinically validated detection of ricin that can be performed by a hospital, healthcare facility, or clinical laboratory. It can go unrecognized as cause of death.

Several assassinations and acts of terror have involved the biological agent ricin. These include the death of Georgi Markov, a Bulgarian dissident who was stabbed by a weaponized umbrella in London; an attack on another Bulgarian defector, Vladimir Kostov; and the poison being mailed to various US politicians (President Barrack Obama, Secretary of Defense James Mattis, and Chief of Naval Operations Admiral John Richardson, among them).

But who would target a clown?

Barffy had no political connections. No reason to be assassinated like spies or terrorists or revolutionists. He just made people laugh with his red-nosed naïf act, bumbling about the big top's center ring, sniffing at everything as if he were a human bloodhound.

~ ~ ~

Rather than deliver the test results over the phone, Doc arranged to meet the police chief at the Cozy Café. At this time of day, the diner offered a degree of privacy. Besides, Doc liked the coffee.

"Got the results, huh?" Chief Purdue greeted the part-time coroner.

"You bet. Just like we thought – poison."

"What kind?"

"Something called ricin."

"Wasn't that what was used in that Japanese subway attack back in '95?"

"Naw, that was sarin. A poisonous gas. Another nasty piece of business."

"Where does one get this ricin?"

"You won't find it on the shelf at Kupnick's Pharmacy. But you can buy the ingredients to make it – castor-oil beans – online."

"Wouldn't that be illegal?" asked the Police Chief.

"Purchasing the seeds to grow a castor oil plant is not illegal, but extracting ricin from the beans is. But who's to know if you do it at home on your kitchen table. All you need are beans and a coffee grinder."

~ ~ ~

Maisie Walters phoned Maddy right away. She often proved to be a good source of information. Waitresses are practically invisible to diners as they talk over a meal.

"Jim and Doc just met for coffee. Doc was giving him the toxicology results – the second round that looked for a rare poison."

"Did they find anything?"

"You bet," she told her sister. "A poison called Rice-A-Roni or something like that."

"Hmm. Could it have been ricin? That's a dangerous poison that comes from the seeds of the castor-oil plant."

"Castor oil? My mom – my adoptive mom, that is – used to give me castor oil all the time. Wonder I'm not dead."

"Castor oil is often used as a laxative."

"I had potty training issues."

"TMI, Sis."

"Oh, okay."

"Thanks for the heads-up."

~ ~ ~

Maddy researched it on Wikipedia:

Castor oil is commonly used orally to relieve constipation. Also, it is used in food additives, flavorings, candy as a mold inhibitor. Castor oil has been used in cosmetic products such as creams and moisturizers. It has been used as a coating in the polyurethane industry. And it has proved useful as a lubricant in jet, diesel, and racing engines.

Also, she knew, parents sometimes use a dose of castor oil to punish naughty children. *Yuck*!

~ ~ ~

"Ricin," said Maddy.

"Ricin?" repeated Lizzie.

"What's that?" echoed Bootsie.

"Ricin is a poison found naturally in castor beans," cited Cookie, drawing on her super memory. "If castor beans are chewed and swallowed, the released ricin can cause serious injury."

"Ricin can be made from the waste material left over from processing castor oil," said Maddy. She'd learned that from her online research.

"Any place around here that processes castor oil beans?" asked Bootsie. Agriculture was not her strong point.

"Not likely," replied Cookie. "The castor plant is indigenous to the southeastern Mediterranean, Ethiopia, and India. A member of the spurge family, it is grown commercially for pharmaceutical and industrial uses. Also, its ornamental flowers are popular in landscaping. The plants can grow 20 or 30 feet tall."

"How does one administer a lethal dose of ricin?" Lizzie posed the question.

"Injected, inhaled, or swallowed."

Bootsie spoke up. "Wasn't ricin used by Bulgarian spies to kill that man in London by poking him with an umbrella?"

"Right," nodded Maddy. "I remember that. Back in the '70s."

"The Robert Koch Institute classifies ricin as a potential biological warfare agent," Cookie expounded. "And it's easy to make. You can find the instructions on the Internet."

Maddy sighed. "May as well forget about the poison. Too easy to obtain. But the question remains, who would want to kill Barffy the Clown?

CHAPTER TWENTY-EIGHT

What Was the Motive?

Maddy gave it some thought: The second toxicology report proved that Barffy the Red-Nosed Clown had been poisoned. Or more specifically, murdered. The Quilters Club's instincts had been (forgive the pun) dead on.

The question remained, who killed him? And why?

What was the motive?

A brainstorming session turned up lots of conflicting ideas – A clown who was jealous over Barffy's success. A dispute over gambling debts. A spurned girlfriend. Someone who had been wronged by the malicious clown. A nut job who simply hated clowns.

None of these had any known facts behind them.

Being a stay-at-home housewife, Maddy had more time to contemplate these alternatives than her three compatriots. Cookie had a demanding job at the Historical Society. Lizzie was overseeing the Quilting Museum. And Bootsie was busily rescuing dogs and cats and hamsters.

Looking for answers, she took these disparate theories to Barffy's manager, Col. Oscar Owensby. The old reprobate was still staying at Hotel Sieur de LaSalle, so Maddy drove over to Burpyville to meet with him. She'd phoned ahead, but he still kept her waiting twenty minutes in the hotel's ornate lobby.

Laying out the various theories, she asked his opinion. "You knew him best," she explained her visit.

"Yes, I suppose I did. But your motives don't hold up."

"Pray tell," she urged him on.

So he ticked them off, one by one, counting on his fingertips.

•Col. Owensby opined that a clown called Topsy the Green Goblin was Barffy's biggest competitor. But he pointed out that Kyle Brownell A/K/A Topsy was a hopeless drunk, not likely to be hired by Ringling Bros. as its lead clown. "Kyle would be wasting his time – and a thimbleful of good poison – to kill Barffy," he waved the idea away.

•The Colonel confirmed that Walter Bradford didn't gamble, other than buying weekly Lottery tickets. "He was too parsimonious," was the man's snide comment. "He had the first penny he ever made."

•At 72, Bradford had three ex-wives, but no current girlfriend. "Two of his former wives have passed away; and he gets along with the surviving ex," he said. "No motive there, because there's not much for her to inherit. He left everything to the Shriners."

•"Possibly it was someone who had a grudge," admitted the Colonel, "given Walt's quarrelsome personality. But nobody stands out."

•"Nut jobs are difficult to anticipate," the Colonel pointed out. "However, such an attack is unlikely. The police say they searched social media for any threats or warning signs, but found nothing."

"So who killed your client?" Maddy put it to Col. Owensby.

"Beats me."

"How about yourself?"

"Lord knows I thought about killing him myself about once a week," he shrugged. "Walt was a very difficult guy to get along with, but he was my Golden Goose. I've managed him since he graduated from Clown College in '81. That's been over 40 years. Little late in the day for me to do him in, wouldn't you say?"

~ ~ ~

What was it Sherlock Holmes said? Sissy reminded herself: "*When you have eliminated the impossible, whatever remains, however improbable, must be the truth.*"

She found it impossible to believe Dorothy Starcatcher had stolen her winning ticket. But the librarian had turned up at the Mayor's Office with the little yellow stub in hand. Highly improbable, to say the least.

The more Sissy thought about it, the more certain she was that she had not dropped the ticket at the library's front desk. She was careful with her purse. But somehow that ticket numbered 756F9K had found its way from her purse into Miss Starcatcher's hands. How could that happen?

Then she thought of the Great Wizardini Magic Room at the back of the library. She had spent many hours there watching the old magician do his feats of legerdemain – pulling quarters from behind kids' ears, finding the Ace of Spades in your pocket, producing items from your wallet, stealing the wristwatch right off your arm.

Hm, if The Great Wizardini could pick your pocket, why not his niece? Couldn't that old dog have taught her a few new tricks?

Still it was hard to accept, that the librarian had stolen the ticket right out of her purse while she stood at the front counter paying for an overdue book.

Of course, this scenario posed another question. How did Dorothy Starcatcher even know she'd had the winning number?

CHAPTER TWENTY-NINE

The Prodigal Son Returns

N'yen came home for a long weekend. The Vietnamese boy said it was because the school's observatory was closed for repairs, but everyone knew it was really because he wanted to visit his girlfriend.

Located on the Evanston campus of Northwestern University, the Dearborn Observatory is considered a "must-stop spot for stargazers." Constructed in 1888, it is equipped with one of the few remaining refracting telescopes (one that uses a lens) in use. Apparently, the lens of the 18.5-inch diameter telescope needed a little polishing.

The observatory dome had been replaced in 1997. The Richardsonian Romanesque style building underwent a complete exterior restoration in 2016/2017. Everyone knows the school takes good care of this astronomical asset.

As an Astrophysics major, N'yen spent most of his waking hours at the powerful telescope. He'd discovered two new quasars now, an impressive accomplishment for someone so young. One had been named after him.

Although N'yen's parents lived in Chicago, he considered Caruthers Corners his second home. His grandparents kept a room for him there. Truth be known, he spent more time in the little Indiana town than he did in Chicago.

N'yen was prepared for Sissy's emotional turmoil. After all, they talked by phone or texted daily. However, smart as he was, he was stumped by this conundrum involving her winning ticket for the Crazy Carnival Quilt. All he could do was follow his cousin Aggie's advice and say, "There, there" – although he was unsure what good that did.

He found her story about Dorothy Starcatcher stealing the ticket from her purse using some kind of slight-of-hand trick to be a bit preposterous. The librarian was on the side of the ledger with The Good Guys. She would never do anything like that … would she?

"Quit defending her," ordered Sissy. "Just accept that she filched my ticket. The question now is how did she know I had it? I didn't tell anybody but Maddy."

"That's easy," he replied. "If Grammy's the only person you told, she must of let it slip to Miss Starcatcher."

But when confronted, Maddy assured them that she hadn't spoken to the librarian that morning.

"You had to have told someone," N'yen insisted.

The silver-hair woman paused to think. "Th only person I spoke with was Cookie. I might have mentioned it to her."

With a snap of his fingers, N'yen came up with a possible chain of conversation. "You told Cookie. And she works with Mary Alice Hegler. Maybe Mary Alice mentioned it to her niece who works in the Library wing next door to the Historical Society."

"Possible," agreed Maddy.

"And so when I waltzed into the Library that morning, Dorothy Starcatcher was ready for me."

"Right," nodded N'yen. "She had at least two of the three elements of The Crime Triangle."

"Crime Triangle?" said Sissy. "What' that?"

"The three factors required to create a criminal offense: Means, Motive, and Opportunity. She had the Means – pickpocketing skills – and the Opportunity – you showing up to pay a library fine. But what was her Motive?"

"She wanted the quilt."

"Bad enough to brazenly steal your ticket and claim it? She would know you'd be onto her, turning up with your ticket."

"Yeah, that's hard to figure."

Maddy summed it up. "To solve this puzzle, we need to figure out why she wanted the quilt badly enough to steal your ticket."

"That's what Aggie said," declared Sissy.

"My granddaughter's a smart girl."

"Aunt Cookie works with Mary Alice," N'yen pointed out. "Maybe she can ferret out the answer."

"Hold on," Maddy said. "I'll phone Cookie right this minute. Get her on the case."

"I don't want this getting back to Miss Starcatcher," whined Sissy.

Maddy *tsk*ed, "Dear girl, at some point we will have to confront her."

~ ~ ~

Despite it being Saturday, Cookie Bentley was in her office at the Historical Society trying to catch up on paperwork. Despite her oh-so-orderly mind, she always kept a messy desk. Papers piled everywhere. "I can't talk right now," she whispered into the phone when she heard the subject. "Mary Alice is here helping me. Give me a few minutes. I'll see what I can find out."

"Okay," replied Maddy, her own voice dropping into a whisper. "We'll talk later."

"What did she say?" asked Sissy. She and N'yen had heard only one side of the conversation.

"That she's on the case."

~ ~ ~

N'yen and Sissy were playing kissy-face in his room when the call from Cookie Bentley came in. Maddy knocked politely on his door to avoid catching them *in flagrante delicto*.

"Mary Alice confirmed that she mentioned your winning the quilt to her niece," his grandmother reported. "So that settles that."

"Oh my goodness, I hope Aunt Cookie didn't let it slip that we were asking about it," said Sissy. "I don't want to tip our hand."

"What hand?" responded her boyfriend. "Aren't we going to confront her, tell her we know she stole your ticket?"

"Not yet," begged Sissy. "She'd just deny it. We need some proof. Maybe find out why she did it."

"*Then* we confront her," insisted N'yen. "That's the only way you'll get your quilt back, Honey Bunny."

Honey Bunny?

CHAPTER THIRTY

The Great Debate

The sun was bright as a spotlight on that brisk Monday morning. For the big mayoral debate, a makeshift stage had been erected in front of the Town Hall, allowing the audience to spread out across the greenery of the Town Square. Two lecterns with microphones dominated the wooden platform.

Nobody seemed overly excited by this public debate. The assumption was that Mark Tidemore would be re-elected as mayor by a landslide. Ken Wurgler's candidacy was a joke to most folks. Nobody took him seriously. But democracy dictated that they go through the motions.

A few reporters milled around, taking notes, snapping photos, and preparing to record snippets of the speeches. Lucius Plancus of WZUR jockeyed his enormous bulk closer to the stage, looking to address questions to both candidates. Not to be left out, Penelope Heath of the *Gazette* also had secured a front row position. Darlene Baxter of Channel 4 was also on hand, although she was a weather girl rather than hardcore journalist. And stringer Bob "Flash" Dougan stood to one side, his Nikon at the ready.

As president of the Town Council, Beau Madison had been asked to moderate the debate, but declined due to the incumbent mayor being his son-in-law. In his stead, *Gazette* publisher Justin Nightly agreed to take over the role. He made a brief speech about Freedom of the Press and the value of Public Debate. Everybody clapped politely.

Based on a coin toss, Wurgler spoke first, his voice thin and reedy. His toupee looked like a crow nesting atop his head. He rattled on about protecting jobs, a theme that sounded like one of his recycled Chamber of Commerce talks. He didn't score many points as to why people should vote for him. It didn't help that the wind blew off his toupee at the end of his speech.

Mark the Shark knew he didn't have to oversell. He merely said, "I would be honored to serve another term as your mayor. Let's keep the progress moving forward. Thank you."

End of speech.

The crowd cheered.

~ ~ ~

The Crazy Carnival quilt was still on display in the downstairs lobby of the Town Hall. As a Pictorial Quilt, it was meant to be a wall hanging rather than a bed coverlet. The colors were dazzling, the textures eye-catching, the design one of perfect symmetry. The Quilters Club had outdone themselves with this one.

Lizzie was responsible for most of the impeccable stitching. Cookie had done the design. Bootsie chose the fabrics. Maddy was happy to have been part of the overall construction. It was a patchwork quilt to be proud of.

Following the mayoral debate, Sissy stood there in the lobby, craning her neck to look up at the quilt display. What was there about it that would make Dorothy Starcatcher lie and steal to possess it?

Was there something valuable hidden in the batting? No, the Quilters Club sewed the quilt. They would know if anything was tucked away between the layers of fabric. Aunt Maddy had assured her there was nothing to be found.

Was there a hidden clue in the design? Maybe a map to a pot of gold?

Or a secret message? Or a holy image like the Shroud of Turin? No, Aunt Cookie said it was just a pretty picture of a circus.

Being new, the quilt couldn't have any historic significance. Or be a priceless antique. Or have sentimental value. Aunt Lizzie had stitched it only a month ago.

Sissy had to admit she was stumped.

Later today, Dorothy would be hauling away the prize. Aggie's dad said she was giving it to her uncle and aunt as a decoration for their apartment at the Hoople Senior Living Home up there on the hill overlooking town. Once it was there, it would be lost to the world. Ernst and Mary Alice Hegler never entertained any visitors.

That made Sissy think of the rumors about Dorothy Starcatcher. Her mother had been the Great Wizardini's stage assistant, but the father was unknown. Some people whispered that Wizardini was the actual father. After all, Dorothy had his blue eyes.

When Ernst and his sister moved to the retirement home, they signed their house out near Green Scum Pond over to Dorothy. A pretty generous gift for the daughter of a former employee. But neither Ernst nor his unmarried sister had any children of their own.

However, if Dorothy was the old magician's biological child, that explained a lot. But how to prove it? You'd never get them to sign up for Ancestor.com and take a DNA test.

She wondered if N'yen might have any ideas about that. He was the cleverest boy she'd ever met. And cute.

CHAPTER THIRTY-ONE

Back to School

"Look, I'm going back to school tomorrow," N'yen said that Tuesday morning. "Get me a DNA sample and I'll run the test in the lab when I get back to Northwestern."

"You can do that?"

"No problem. I have a lab pass."

"What kind of sample do you need?"

"You know, the usual. Like you see on TV police shows. A hair follicle, a cigarette, a drinking glass. Something like that."

"If you're going back tomorrow, I've got to work fast."

"I'm not sure how this will help you get your quilt back, but anything for you, Cupcake."

"Cupcake?"

"It's my new term of endearment for you. I'll be trying out several to see which one sticks. Being in a committed relationship, I think we should have affectionate nicknames, don't you?"

Sissy gave it a moment's thought. "Yes, that's a good idea … Snuggle Bug."

~ ~ ~

Sissy's opportunity came that very afternoon. N'yen was off fishing with his Grampy and Uncle Edgar, a last-minute outing before returning to school. She had bicycled to the Dollar General on South Main to pick up some Ziploc bags to hold any DNA samples she might collect. That's when she spotted Ernst and Mary Alice Hegler having DQ Blizzards with Dorothy Starcatcher. Sitting at the concrete table in front of the Dairy Queen, they were the picture of a perfect family outing, each slurping from a large plastic cup.

Hmm.

Parking her bike, Sissy sauntered across the street to Kupnick's Pharmacy. It was open late on Tuesday nights. She pretended to be looking at nail polish while the Heglers finished off their frozen custards. Phil Kupnick was pretty tolerant about kids hanging around his Rexall. He did a good fountain business despite being directly across the street from the Dairy Queen and Cozy Café. Young people hereabouts has a sweet tooth, he liked to say.

When the trio across the street tossed their plastic cups in the trash bin and ambled off, she hurried over and retrieved the three items for her Ziploc bags. She used a pencil to juggle the containers into her plastic bags, careful not to contaminate them with her own DNA.

The idea had been to get samples from Ernst Hegler and his so-called niece, but Sissy couldn't tell which two had been theirs, so she brought along all three. N'yen could sort them out with his miraculous lab techniques, she told herself.

~ ~ ~

Beau Madison and Edgar Ridenour co-owned a boat – a 20-foot Roughneck 2070 SC – that they used to traverse the Wabash, fishing for catfish and largemouth bass. N'yen joined them when he was around. The boy was the better fisherman of the three. He'd caught (and released) Big Calvin, the giant catfish who lurked near the Highway 101 Bridge. Now they were pursuing a new adversary, a humongous bass known as The Monster.

Today, they lolled at the bend in the river near Injun Woods, that campsite belonging to the Sons of Anthony Wayne, an organization founded in 1978 by the late Hank Warton as a protest against the Boy Scouts of America relocating its headquarters to Texas. Edgar had spotted The Monster in the shallow waters near the bend.

Although cargo ships used to traverse the Wabash, silt and mud had all but clogged the waterway. Fortunately, the Roughneck had a shallow draft.

The aluminum Jon boat with a variable deadrise Modified Vee hull delivered a remarkably smooth and dry ride. The side-console layout was easy to drive, with N'yen usually taking the helm when he went along on one of the excursions up the river. The Mercury engine provided lots of power.

The trio often argued over how to catch The Monster. Bass generally prefer warm, shallow parts of reservoirs, lakes, and rivers. Their bucket-size big mouth allows them to eat everything from tiny zooplankton to mice and snakes. But bass can be fooled by lures causing naturalistic flashes or quick movements.

"I like to use a small rubber bait that imitates baitfish. Known as a fluke, it was first introduced by the Zoom Bait Company, but now hundreds of imitators offer replacements," said Edgar.

"Me, I prefer the Senko," said N'yen. "It's pretty easy to fish. And there are many ways to rig it."

"Yes," replied his grandfather, "but the bite is subtle. It generally has to be worked very slowly."

"For new anglers, that's hard to do," his Uncle Edgar pointed out.

"Hey, I'm not a new angler. Who was it that caught Big Calvin?"

"Hey, don't brag."

The conversation drifted from fishing to local gossip to the dead clown.

"Why is Grammy and the Quilters Club so eager to solve this case?" asked the boy.

"Because of me," answered Beau. "The death of Barffy closed down the carnival. That's a big financial loss for the town."

"How's that your fault?"

"The carnival was my idea. If Ken Wurgler wins the mayor's race, he will move to fire me as president of the Town Council."

Edgar spoke up. "If he does that, we councilmen will all resign – me, Ben, Jim, maybe some others."

"Now, now, let's cross that bridge when we come to it. But that's why Maddy is so determined to solve the clown's death. As a reprieve for me."

"Don't worry, Grampy. Have faith in the Quilters Club. They'll find that green-haired clown who killed Barffy. They make Sam Spade look like an inept piker."

"Here's looking at you, kid," said Beau, tipping an imaginary hat. "Let's hope you're right."

~ ~ ~

Waiting for N'yen to return from fishing, Sissy cranked up her computer and did a little research on DNA:

Deoxyribonucleic acid is a self-replicating polymer molecule that carries the genetic instructions for the development, growth, and reproduction found in every living organism.

Commonly known as DNA, these genetic markers allow this information to be passed from one generation to the next. Each person's genetic profile is unique.

There was more:

DNA Profiling is the forensic technique used in criminal investigations to compare DNA evidence to determine someone's involvement in a crime.

DNA Paternity Testing is the use of DNA profiles to determine whether an individual is the biological parent of another individual. Because DNA is passed down from both parents 50/50 to their children, results are obtained by comparing a DNA sample from the child, mother, and alleged father.

Each one of us is born with a unique genetic blueprint. With current technology, DNA Paternity Tests have an accuracy of over 99.99%.

"Here you go ... Snookums," said Sissy, handing her boyfriend a paper sack containing the three Ziploc bags. "Those DNA samples you needed."

"Already? How did you manage that?" He tossed his fishing gear onto the mudroom floor and peered into the paper sack.

"Easy as pie. Dorothy Starcatcher is not the only clever person around here," she replied with a self-satisfied smile.

CHAPTER THIRTY-TWO

Slight-of-Hand

Twentysome years ago, The Great Wizardini had been a popular stage magician widely known for his close-up magic. These are tricks performed in an intimate setting usually no more than 10 feet from one's audience. Sometimes it's called sleight-of-hand or prestidigitation ("quick fingers") or *léger de main* (French for "lightness of hand").

While most magic uses misdirection to produce an illusion, close-up magic is more of a straightforward display of skill, comparable to juggling or pickpocketing.

As everyone knows, pickpocketing is stealing money or other valuables from a victim's pocket without the theft being noticed at the time. It involves considerable dexterity – similar to that used by a magician. Many magicians feature it in their act. Illusionist David Avadon calls it "the underground art."

An open secret among magicians was a group known as the Artful Dodgers, professional magicians who formed a pickpocketing ring in the late '90s. Back in the 18th and 19th Century, most pickpockets stole out of economic need; but these sticky-fingered rogues did it strictly for sport.

The Great Wizardini had been a member of the Artful Dodgers.

~ ~ ~

Dorothy's mother – Stella Starcatcher – was The Great Wizardini's stage assistant; Dorothy's father was unknown. After her mother's premature death, Dorothy had been raised by Ernst Hegler and his sister Mary Alice.

Mostly she spent her youth in boarding schools. The Great Wizardini was always on the road, performing in one small town after another. Mary Alice was the Caruthers Corners Librarian for many years, more recently becoming the Historic Society's archivist.

When home from his tours, The Great Wizardini taught the girl magic tricks – The False Cut, Palming, The Elmsley Count, The Riffle Force, The Double Lift. And Mary Alice instructed her in the Dewey Decimal System, Library of Congress Classification, and cataloguing techniques.

Dorothy became a librarian.

Now she headed up the Caruthers Corners Public Library, located in a wing of the Perricock Science and History Museum.

She was also a skilled pickpocket.

Ernst had taught this sticky-fingers proficiency to his niece. He was proud to say she was a natural.

~ ~ ~

The next morning N'yen drove back to school, his little Volkswagen spewing smoke like an out-of-tune lawnmower. If he got there on schedule, he could book lab time tomorrow. He'd never done DNA sequencing before, but he had seen it done. That was usually enough for him to emulate a procedure. After all, his IQ was "through the roof," as one psychologist had proclaimed.

He wished he had a sample of Stella Starcatcher's DNA, but that ship had sailed. The Great Wizardini's one-time stage assistant had died twenty years ago. Rumor said Wizardini had accidentally sawed her in half, but nobody really believed that story.

But with a little luck, he might be able to connect Dorothy with The Great Wizardini if Ernst Hegler was indeed her father.

CHAPTER THIRTY-THREE

Fright Night

School took up a lot of Sissy's time, what with her classes and after-hours activities. But she was a hard worker. Not being a genius like her boyfriend, she made extra efforts to keep up.

Sissy had been spending hours on end practicing the songs from *My Fair Lady*. That was the next play coming up. Auditions would take place next month. But she wasn't sure Caruthers High was ready for a black Eliza Doolittle. The recent "colorblind" casting of *My Fair Lady* had been an aberration.

Fortunately, her grandfather was a tad hard of hearing. He never complained about her rehearsing in her bedroom. Or maybe it was because his bedroom was on the other side of the house from hers.

Buck Jackson may have enjoyed his granddaughters vocalizations, but there's only so many repetitions of "Wouldn't It Be Loverly" and "I Could Have Danced All Night" that one human being can take.

Tonight, giving her voice a rest, she decided to look more closely into clowns – particularly scary clowns.

Pennywise was easy. She watched DVDs of the Tim Curry version of *It* (2009) and the two Bill Skarsgård versions (2017 and 2019). That Stephen King was a master at writing horror stories.

She couldn't help but shudder as she loaded the DVDs into her Sony player. Tonight was going to be a marathon that would make Elvira, Mistress of the Dark, proud.

Another clown you wouldn't want to meet in a dark alley was Captain Spaulding. Played by character actor Sid Haig, he was a mass murderer created by Rob Zombie for his horror movies: *House of 1000 Corpses, The Devil's Rejects*, and *3 from Hell*. Taking the name from a Groucho Marx character, Captain Spaulding is the proprietor of a gas station/fried chicken establishment in Texas. There's also a haunted house attraction on the property: Captain Spaulding's Museum of Monsters and Madmen, which features a ride-through exhibit with jarred fetuses and photos of serial killers.

Still another, *Clown Town* (2016) told about a group of friends who are stranded in a small town where they are stalked by psychopaths dressed as clowns.

Also, there was Art the Clown who was the main antagonist in several films: *All Hallow's Eve* (2013), *Terrifier* (2011), and *Terrifier 2* (2022). A demonic killer clown in a black-and-white costume and face paint, Art comes out on Halloween nights with a black trash bag filled with weapons.

Of course, there were those *Killer Klowns from Outer Space* (1988). And that clown puppet in Steven Spielberg's *Poltergeist* (1982). And *Stitches* (2012), the story of a clown who comes back from the dead.

There were so many. *Killjoy; The Clown at Midnight; The Clown Murders; 31; Scary or Die; The Last Circus* ... on and on and on.

Sissy didn't have time to watch them all. Not that they were all available on the Redbox at Kupnick's Pharmacy. Time to get some sleep. It was 2 in the morning.

~ ~ ~

Beau Madison decided not to go fishing today. This was to his pal Edgar's disappointment. Edgar was out to catch that bass they had dubbed The Monster. He'd spotted the fish a couple of time near Injun Woods; it would measure over 20 inches, he estimated.

Typical length for a largemouth bass (*Micropterus salmoides*) is 5 to 10 inches, with the longest recorded specimen being 38.2 inches. The heaviest reported weight for a largemouth is 22 pounds 5 ounces. The record in Indiana was 14 pounds 12 inches. He was sure The Monster would top that.

Instead of a day on the Wabash, Beau decided he would drive over to Burpyville to see his old friend, Judge Horace Cramer. These days the judge was usually found in his office at the Burpyville Courthouse, although he still maintained a satellite office in Caruthers Corners.

Judge Cramer raised beagles at his farm up Highway 73 toward Swisstown. They were fine hunting stock, prized by anyone lucky enough to get a pup. Edgar didn't own a dog, but the judge loaned him one when he went hunting.

Beau found Horace Cramer eating lunch at his desk. A tuna sandwich with pickles. The jurist waved Beau in and offered to share his sandwich, but his pal waved him off. "No thanks. I had a late breakfast at Maisie's."

"Lucky dog. Cozy Café makes better tuna sandwiches than these I get at the Courthouse Diner."

"You're spending too much time at this office. You've got a perfectly good workspace over in Caruthers Corners."

"True, but I've been spending more time in court lately. Got too many legal wranglings going on. Bet you've brought me one too."

"As it happens, I'm looking for advice."

"Got plenty of that."

"Well, as you know, Mark has an opponent in the upcoming mayoral election."

"That idiot Ken Wurgler. I wouldn't worry about him."

"Problem is, I know something about Ken. Just don't know if I should act on it or let things take their course."

"Dirt?"

"Kinda. He's been skimming from the Chamber of Commerce budget. Not much, but not proper."

"You want to know whether to use it against him in the election?"

"Guess I do. Technically, he's broke the law, but in normal times I'd just slap him on the hand, make him reimburse it and promise not to do it again."

"That seems reasonable. As you know, I'm not a hanging judge. I can turn a blind eye to minor infractions. And matters settled privately don't take up my time in court."

"So I shouldn't use it against him in the mayor's race?"

"You don't really need to, in my opinion. Ken doesn't have a snowball's chance in Miami of getting elected."

"Thanks for your time, Horace."

"One of my beagles just had pups. Want one?"

"Might be interested. Aggie's gonna take her dog back to New Haven at Christmas. And we're kinda used to having a mutt around."

Judge Cramer nodded. "Come pick him out. But he's a purebred beagle. Don't you go calling him a mutt."

CHAPTER THIRTY-FOUR

The DNA Results

Sissy was having dinner at the Madison house that night – a common happenstance – when she got the call from N'yen. "Excuse me," she got up from the table. "This is very important."

"My grandson?" said Maddy.

"Could be," the girl said evasively. She was still embarrassed by all this lovey-dovey stuff.

Case in point, it gave her pause when N'yen greeted her, "Hi, Buttercup."

"I thought I was 'Cupcake'," she replied.

"I told you I'm trying out terms of endearment. Today it's 'Buttercup.' "

"Okay, uh, Honey Bunch."

"That's it. You're getting the hang of this."

"Did you get any results from the DNA test?" she changed the subject. She could feel her cheeks getting red. Didn't want the Madisons to witness her embarrassment. Buttercup, indeed.

"That's what I'm calling about. But the results are not what I expected."

"You mean Dorothy isn't the Great Wizardini's daughter?"

"No, she is. But something else. I had to run the DNA on all three cups, not knowing which was which. And it turns out, Mary Alice Hegler is her mother."

"Holy cow, are we talking incest here – like with the Crackletons?"

"No. Turns out, Ernst and Mary Alice are not brother and sister. But they *are* Dorothy's parents."

"Ooo, that's juicy. But it doesn't explain why Dorothy Starcatcher wants that quilt so badly."

"The answer's not apparent. But I'm sure it's here somewhere," said N'yen.

"I think we need some help from the Quilters Club," she whispered into the phone. "Don't you agree … Cutie Pie?"

~ ~ ~

The four women gathered around Sissy Jackson, stunned at her news. What she'd just revealed about Ernst and Mary Alice Hegler had left them speechless. When the girl had called an emergency meeting of the Quilters Club, they had expected nothing like this.

Maddy recovered her voice first. "You're saying that Ernst and Mary Alice are Dorothy's parents?" Having been a secret love child herself, Maddy could deal with the twisted branches of a family tree.

"*I'm* not saying that," protested Sissy. "That's what the DNA says. N'yen ran the tests himself at his school lab."

"Is he qualified to do that?" asked Lizzie dubiously.

"He's an astrophysics major in the graduate school at Northwestern University. And a certified genius. Let's give him some credit," she defended her boyfriend.

"For the time being, let's take those test results at face value," said Maddy. She had confidence in her grandson. "We have to figure out what it means. And does it have anything to do with Dorothy stealing Sissy's ticket."

"Very well, let's review the facts," suggested Cookie. She had such an orderly mind. Her memory worked like a room filled with filing cabinets.

"Fact one," said Maddy. "Sissy had the winning ticket for our quilt. I saw it myself."

"Thank you," sighed Sissy. Appreciative for the confirmation.

"Fact two, Dorothy Starcatcher now has the winning ticket. She showed it to Mark the Shark," Bootsie joined in. "That means she either found it or stole it."

Lizzie spoke up. "Fact three, Dorothy plans to give the quilt to Ernst and Mary Alice Hegler. At least that's what she told Mark."

"Fact four," added Maddy. "Ernst and Mary Alice are Dorothy's biological parents."

"Wait," said Cookie. "Let's stop right there for a moment. Do a sidebar. Examine Dorothy's parentage."

"How old is she?" asked Lizzie.

"I saw her application for the library position," replied Maddy. "Mark wanted my opinion about hiring her. She was 37 at the time. 38 now."

"That means she was born in 1984," Cookie did the instant calculation.

"So she was conceived around 1983. Let's assume Ernst and Mary Alice got married about then. Is there any marriage certificate?"

"We'd have to research that," said Cookie. "I can't recall documents I've not seen."

Maddy nodded. "I'd suggest we look in the records at the Burpyville courthouse as a start. I'd guess Ernst is from around here. Hegler is a common name in this part of Indiana."

"Anything significant about the year 1983?" asked Bootsie.

"Let me see," said Cookie, running through newspaper files in her mind like reels of microfiche. "Hmm, the space shuttle Challenger was launched that year. *Stern* magazine published those phony Hitler diaries. The world's first commercial mobile phone call was made. US troops invaded Grenada. There was a solar eclipse on December 4th."

"Anything closer to home?"

Cookie shifted her timeline. "The Lost Boys wandered off into Never Ending Swamp in 1982. Aitkins Produce had a bumper watermelon crop in '83. The Albanese Candy Company started manufacturing gummies that year. And only time ever, the Indiana State Fair was held in multiple locations."

"I remember that," said Maddy. "Due to renovations at the Indiana State Fairground, the fair was split into ten locations across the state that year."

Lizzie piped in. "One of those locations was here in Caruthers Corners. I remember going. We were home from college by then."

"I thought the State Fair was always held in Indianapolis," said Sissy.

"There have been exceptions," responded Bootsie. "Just ask your Aunt Cookie. I'm sure she can give the details."

"That's right. Other Indiana cities have hosted the State Fair from time to time," cited Cookie. "Those alternates locations have included Lafayette in 1853; Madison in 1854; New Albany in 1859; Fort Wayne in 1865; Terre Haute in 1867, and multiple towns in 1983. There was no fair 1917 and 1918 due to World War I nor from 1942 to 1944 because of

World War II. Otherwise, it has been held at the Indiana State Fairgrounds since 1892."

"Yes," remembered Lizzie. "In 1983 a part of the State Fair took place in our Town Square. It's only ten acres, twenty if you count the space south of town that it spilled onto."

Cookie chimed in. "The Indiana State Fairgrounds covers 214 acres, 72 buildings, a 6,000-seat grandstand, and a racetrack. That's why they had to spread it over ten other locations while the original site was being renovated."

"My mom and dad got married at the Indiana State Fair back in 1950," reminisced Bootsie. She could get very nostalgic. She had a soft place in her heart for her late parents. "Getting married at the fair's a popular thing to do. Normandy Barn on the Fairgrounds is a big wedding venue, offering event planners, on-site catering, and reception facilities."

"Do you think Ernst and Mary Alice got married at the State Fair in Caruthers Corners?"

"Could be. That might be why Dorothy wanted our quilt. It pictured a fair like the one where her parents were wed. Maybe it's kind of an anniversary gift."

"But the dates don't match," argued Cookie. "This carnival took place in the fall. The State Fair is always in the summer."

"A belated anniversary gift?" Maddy guessed. Nobody had any better ideas.

"But stealing my ticket to get it was a pretty rotten thing to do," groused Sissy.

"Agreed," nodded Bootsie, her sense of justice offended. That came with being a policeman's wife. "I'm very disappointed in Dorothy."

"Me too," said Lizzie.

"One thing doesn't make sense," worried Maddy. "If Ernst and Mary Alice were married, why keep it a secret? And why not acknowledge that they are Dorothy's parents? Why give her the stigma of being illegitimate?"

"Good question," acknowledged Bootsie.

"Yeah, I have no idea," echoed Lizzie.

"Let's go ask them," suggested Cookie. "Quit beating around the bush."

"But we don't have any real proof," hesitated Sissy. "What if we're wrong?"

"The facts are on our side," insisted Cookie. "There's no doubt Dorothy stole your ticket. Time to confront her."

"I agree," nodded Maddy. "It's time Dorothy Starcatcher explained her actions. She's been behaving like a common garden-variety sneak thief."

"Oh my," groaned Sissy. "I'll never be able to go to the library again."

CHAPTER THIRTY-FIVE

No Nuptials

"The answer is simple," said Ernst Hegler. "Mary Alice and I were never married. Dorothy was illegitimate. My assistant Stella agreed to play surrogate; Mary Alice and I would pretend to be siblings; my career wouldn't be damaged. In retrospect, it was the wrong thing to do, not fair to Dorothy. But there you are."

"Then why the sentimentality over our quilt?"

"It was an anniversary present," said Dorothy Starcatcher. Her eyes downcast with embarrassment.

"That's right," nodded her father. "Mary Alice and I met at the 1983 State Fair. Dorothy knew we treasured that memory. It's where she was conceived. Perhaps she went overboard in trying to support our sense of nostalgia."

"You darn tootin' " sniffed Sissy Jackson. "She stole my quilt."

"Guess I did," admitted Dorothy Starcatcher. "My dear, I give you my very sincere apology. And I'll submit my resignation as town librarian to the mayor first thing tomorrow."

"Maybe that's not necessary," said Maddy, showing surprising compassion. "You're a good librarian. You made a mistake. Let's hope you learned something from it."

"What about my quilt?" pressed Sissy.

"Here's the deal," said Cookie, brushing her blonde hair out of her face. It was overdue for a trim. She wasn't a regular at Helen of Troy. "You get your quilt back. And the second one we were doing for you will go to the Heglers instead."

"That's right," affirmed Maddy with a broad smile. "Everybody will get a quilt."

"Oh, thank you," cooed Mary Alice. "That means so much to us."

"I hope we're not asking too much," said Ernst, "but could you continue to keep our secret?"

"About being Dorothy's parents?"

"That, and about me and Mary Alice not being brother and sister."

"Why not come clean?'

"We're comfortable with the *status quo*," said Mary Alice.

Ernst nodded his agreement. "We need no scandal."

"Okay, your secret is safe with us," said Lizzie. "We promise we'll never tell."

"Lizzie!" everybody squealed in unison. It was well-known that the redhead was an inveterate gossip, unable to keep even the smallest secret. The poster girl for "loose lips..."

"Honest," Lizzie affirmed, holding up her hand as if taking an oath.

Nobody looked convinced.

"Do your best," said The Great Wizardini.

"What?"

"Do your best."

"Uh, do my best?"

"Do your best," he repeated smoothly. It sounded like a magical incantation. Or a hypnotic suggestion.

Either way, Lizzie nodded obediently.

~ ~ ~

Many of the Crackletons had worked in carnival sideshows from time to time. Easy money for those with interesting afflictions. Where else could you make a quick buck by showing off your lobster paw or extra limb or giant height? Randolph and Rex enjoyed amazing the rubes with their extra eyeballs.

Sideshows became a popular add-on to circuses in the late 19th Century. P.T. Barnum was a major influence on the popularity of sideshows, having demonstrated their attraction at his American Museum. His shows included "human abnormalities, such as fat ladies, giants and dwarfs, armless wonders, and four-legged girls; illusions and magicians; automatons and curious inventions; and various works of art ...."

Relegated to its own string of tents, the Freak Show was always festooned with giant banners illustrating the human marvels inside. A "talker" lured customers by ballyhooing the unbelievable sights to be found within the tent. With his loud baritone voice, Jeb Crackleton usually took on this huckster role for his family. Being a giant, people usually stopped to listen to his spiel.

Three Eyes Johnson had been promoted as the main draw for the Crazy Carnival's sideshow. His extra oculus was a curiosity rarely encountered – not to say that pinheads and werewolves and lobster-claw boys were common sights.

Crackleton Crossing had plenty of such oddities, but paying your 50¢ to see them as sideshow exhibits was less embarrassing than staring wide-eyed from the window of your passing car at the Crossing. Looking was okay when they invited you to do it. Paying a token fee lessened the guilt that came with a guilty pleasure.

Three Eyes didn't mind people's curiosity about his unique appearance. He and Rex were used to it. They liked the attention.

CHAPTER THIRTY-SIX

A Redo

"**I** want a redo," whined Ken Wurgler. He was standing timidly in front of the Caruthers Corners Town Council, pleading for a second debate.

"A redo?" said Beau. "This is not a game of marbles where you flubbed your shot." As president of the Town Council, he was presiding over the meeting in the upstairs conference room at the Town Hall.

"Ain't fair," Ken continued to wheedle. "Mark ambushed me with that short speech. Made mine look like diarrhea of the mouth. You know I have a tendency to talk too much."

"True," nodded Beau. "But it was your choice to drone on and on about job creation. Seemed a bit of overkill, considering most people around here are fully employed. Anybody who isn't, Aitkens Produce can always use more watermelon pickers."

"What about those shiftless Crackletons?" replied Ken. "Half of them don't work."

"They live off larceny," muttered the Police Chief. "But I'm trying to put 'em outta business. Just arrested three smash-and-grab kids yesterday."

"See what I mean? Rampant crime – I didn't get to go into any of that."

"I'm confused," said Edgar. "Do you want a second chance to say more? – or say less?"

"Lots of political campaigns have more than one debate," argued Ken. "Most Presidential debates usually have two or three."

"This is hardly a Presidential debate," said Beau.

"C'mon, fair is fair."

Beau frowned. "You don't deserve a second turn, Ken. I have evidence that you –"

"No need to go into that," Mark signaled his father-in-law to not go into that.

"You gotta give me another chance," the little man raised his voice to a screech. "I demand –"

"Calm down, Ken. We can go again, if you want to," shrugged Mark Tidemore. "I'm always happy to speak to my constituents."

"That's great. My seconds will call on your seconds to arrange a date." He made it sound like a pistol duel at dawn.

~ ~ ~

Beau's old war buddy Buckley Jackson drove over to Pleasant Glades to visit the grave of his late wife. As was his habit, he brought flowers. She had liked chrysanthemums. He liked to talk with her, even if he knew she wasn't there. He liked to think she was in Heaven.

Buck knew she would be proud of their granddaughter, Cecelia. The girl was growing up to be a fine young lady. She had been quite a hit in the school play, that *Sound of Music* musical. She had a wonderful voice.

Her mother had a great singing voice too, but she had gotten sidetracked by drugs. He hadn't heard from her in several years.

He was happy to have custody of Cecilia, to share a home with her. Not that she was there a lot. School took up a lot of time, especially her extracurricular activities. And she spent a lot of time at the Madison house on Melon Pickers Row. He approved of that. Beau and Maddy were like a second family to her. And their granddaughter Aggie was her best friend. Not to mention their grandson N'yen being her boyfriend. He came down from college at least once a month. They seemed pretty serious.

He liked to tell his wife about the girl's achievements. She would have enjoyed the stories. And at any rate, he enjoyed telling them, even if no one was listening.

Last week Sissy had won a drawing for a patchwork quilt, one that depicted a circus scene. Something to do with the recent Crazy Carnival that had sprung up like a field of mushrooms in the Town Square. Too bad about that clown getting killed. That kinda spoiled things.

Buck didn't particularly like clowns. They looked like something out of nightmares. He didn't sleep well. He had dreams of Vietnam – PPSD, they called it – even though that war was half a century ago. Fortunately, his friend Beau didn't share that affliction.

Beau used to joke, "I sleep well because my heart is pure." Maybe that was true. Beau was the finest man he'd ever known. That tall drink of water had saved his life in 'Nam. And he'd returned the favor. They had each other's back.

He would be pleased if his granddaughter married into the Madison family. It didn't bother him that N'yen was Vietnamese, those bad memories aside. He was a smart boy, a genius they said. And if Sissy married into the Madison family she'd always have a home. They were "good people."

Buck spread the chrysanthemums in front of the marble headstone like a yellow blanket, said a little prayer, then made

his way back to his junker car parked outside the cemetery
gates.

CHAPTER THIRTY-SEVEN

Green Hair and Ham

Margie Yost finished touching up Lizzie's red hair. Margie herself had blue hair. As proprietor of Helen of Troy Spa & Beauty Salon, she thought her hair color was a good advertisement for the beauty salon's creativity.

Lizzie had been a redhead since high school (thank you, Lady Clairol). She thought it reflected her fiery personality. She had been the most outgoing member of the cheerleading squad, the Girl Most Likely to Shout Back at Supporters of the Visiting Team.

Having graduated from Burpyville Cosmetology & Manicure School, Margie knew that less than 2 percent of the world's population has red hair. "Women who choose to wear very red hair are distinguished by their audacity," she quoted. "Red is the sign of courage, but also of sensuality. Dazzling color par excellence, red is the color of passion and blood. When a person likes red she displays a strong personality."

"That's me," Lizzie nodded. "A strong personality."

However, she might have been less quick to agree if she'd known the history of red hair in the circus.

~ ~ ~

Ancient theatre created a stigma: red hair equaled "clown." Those actors playing the fool had to wear a red-haired wig. You can trace a direct line from characters on the Greek stage to the modern red-haired circus clown and Ronald McDonald.

To differentiate themselves, circus clowns began varying their costumes and wigs and face paint. In the late 1940s a man named Stan Bolt started recording clowns' painted faces on blown eggs. This developed into the Clown Egg Registry, a system which acts like copyright for each clown's individual painted face. There are over 250 eggs in the collection. It is maintained by Clowns International, the oldest clown society in the world.

This egg-based system of registering clowns' makeup designs operates outside the courts and is not overseen by lawyers. But it seems to work.

Protecting a clown's look is difficult. There are an estimated 100,000 professional clowns worldwide. There are even more amateurs.

~ ~ ~

If red hair traditionally represents a good clown, green hair signified a bad clown.

The most famous green-haired clown is Víctor Alberto Trujillo Matamoros (born July 30, 1961). A Mexican actor and comedian, his best-known character is Brozo el Payaso Tenebroso ("Brozo the Creepy Clown") – "a green-haired, unkempt, obscene, and aggressive clown."

Batman's fictional foe, The Joker, also has green hair. As co-creator Bill Finger recalls:

"I got a call from Bob Kane ... He had a new villain. When I arrived he was holding a playing card.

Apparently Jerry Robinson or Bob, I don't recall who, looked at the card and they had an idea for a character ... the Joker. But I remembered the Victor Hugo novel *The Man Who Laughs* — his face had been permanently operated on so that he will always have this perpetual grin. And it looked absolutely weird. I cut the picture out of the book and gave it to Bob, who drew the profile and gave it a more sinister aspect. Then he worked on the face; made him look a little clown-like, which accounted for his white face, red lips, green hair."

And let's not forget those green-haired clowns in the 1988 film *Killer Klowns From Outer Space*. The Killer Klowns were an onslaught of evil extraterrestrials who resembled clowns. After arriving on Earth, they invaded a small town in order to "capture, kill and harvest the human inhabitants to use as sustenance by drinking their blood."

One of the main antagonists, a Killer Klown named Shorty had green hair coming out in three swatches on his head. He wore a yellow suit with stars across the front. Other green-haired Killer Klowns included the massive Jumbo; Fatso's twin; Tall and his two brothers; Bash who has a stripe running through his green hair; and Dunk's various body doubles.

Yes, there are lots of green-haired clowns out there. But only one had been in Barffy's dressing room.

~ ~ ~

"Killer clowns? Where have I heard that before?" muttered Chief Jim Purdue. He had just sat down to dinner at his little cottage off Highway 21 East. His wife had prepared one of his favorite meals – pork chops with watermelon glaze.

"Quit worrying about work and enjoy your food," Bootsie urged. She was trying to mollify her hubby. He was still put out over the Quilters Club muscling in on his case.

"But that phrase rings a bell."

"Of course it does," she said, reminding him that they had seen a movie on Netflix last month called *Killer Klowns from Outer Space*. A silly sci-fi horror flick that Rotten Tomatoes had called "darkly goofy fun."

"Oh yeah, I remember that one. Thought it was pretty stupid," said her husband. "Slept through most of it." He sawed into his thick charbroiled chop, popped it into his mouth, and chewed thoughtfully.

At least he wasn't dealing with aliens from other planets, he told himself. That was something to be thankful for.

CHAPTER THIRTY-EIGHT

Slow Start

"**M**ark phoned me today, asking for a report on our investigation of Barffy's death," Maddy reported to her friends.

"Uh-oh," said Lizzie. "What did you tell him. We've got squat."

"I told him we were still quietly poking around."

"Liar, liar, pants on fire," chided Cookie.

"We are off to a very slow start," Bootsie acknowledged. "The police have been interviewing people, looking under rocks."

"We got sidetracked with Sissy's problem," Maddy admitted. "But with that solved, we can get back on track with the Killer Clown Case, as the *Burpyville Gazette* calls it."

"We better get a move on, or the police will crack the case before we do," urged Bootsie.

"It's not a competition," said Cookie.

"Yes, it is," declared the police chief's wife. There was obviously more going on in the Purdue household than met the eye.

"Everybody calm down," shushed Maddy. "We may be getting off to a late start, but nothing lost. Barffy is still dead."

~ ~ ~

Bootsie's assignment was to find out what the police knew. No need for the Quilters Club to duplicate the cops' efforts, Maddy pointed out.

Nobody doubted that Bootsie could deliver. She had her hubby twisted around her little finger. He couldn't keep secrets from her.

Jim Purdue had a thing for Ruebenesque women. He was as smitten with Barbara Jo Purdue (née Hofstadter) as he was when he first met her in high school. She'd been a pal of Beau Madison's girlfriend, Madelyn Taylor (as she was known back then). They, along with Cookie Johansson and Lizzie Bergamachi, had comprised the cheerleading squad.

Beau, Jim, and Edgar – their future husbands – were first stringers on the football team. Ben was the state wrestling champion.

That next morning Bootsie fixed her husband his favorite breakfast, watermelon waffles and thick slabs of bacon. She knew the way to his secrets was through his stomach. Left to their own appetites, the couple would have looked like Sumo wrestlers. Fortunately, Jenny Craig came to the rescue now and again.

"To what do I owe this pleasure?" said Jim, digging into the stack of waffles. They were topped with whipped cream and syrup. The waffles were chunky with diced watermelon. It was a stack of three, hot off the grill.

"No reason," she lied.

Her husband knew this was a white fib. Between mouthfuls, he mumbled, "What do you want to know?"

"Where are you with the Killer Clown Case?"

"We think a clown with green hair did it. But we're having trouble identifying him." He took another bite, then said,

"Who do you Quilters Clubbers think poisoned that big-nosed clown?"

"Oh, same as you," she bluffed. "A clown with green hair."

"Get any leads?"

"A few, nothing to get excited about."

"Yeah, I know the feeling. Think I could have another batch of waffles?"

CHAPTER THIRTY-NINE

"They're *All* Scary!"

Bootsie reported, "My hubby thinks Barffy was poisoned by the green-hair clown Birdie saw in the dressing room. Based on the message he left, it's clear the guy had a grudge against Barffy. Besides, there are no other likely suspects."

"Okay, our mission is clear," said Lizzie, sitting up straight. Her words were determined. "We need to find a green-haired clown who was at the carnival that night." She had just had her hair dyed (red as usual) at Helen of Troy, a weekly standing appointment – so she had hair color on her mind.

"There are three known candidates," Bootsie reminded her friends. "Billy Tuckman, driver of that clown car; Gary Griffin, the tall member of the Klown Kar Krew; and Kyle Brownell, the scary clown."

"They're *all* scary!" said Lizzie. She gave a little shiver to make her point.

"Kyle Brownell – Topsy, that is – wasn't at the Crazy Carnival," Cookie pointed out. "May as well mark him off the list."

"Not so fast," responded Bootsie. "He worked with the clowns who were there. Harry Teague got his name from that Littleton guy."

"We're going to check the other clowns' alibies," reasoned Maddy. "Adding Topsy won't hurt."

Cookie continued being argumentative. "I thought Harry Teague had already done that."

"Harry's good at his job. But I trust our research more," said Maddy. "Let's backtrack. Make sure he didn't miss anything."

"Oh, okay," the historian gave in. Nobody was more thorough than her.

"Why don't we make it easy," suggested Lizzie. "Each of us take a clown to check?"

"There are three of them – four of us."

"I propose you gals go to Chicago and re-check the alibis of those three clowns," said Maddy. "And I will search for any other green-hair clowns we may have overlooked."

"How could we miss one?" said Cookie. "All the clowns were booked through Littleton & Co. Eric Littleton knows what each one of them looks like – green hair or not."

"Not Freddie. He was there."

"Your son is not a suspect," said Lizzie. "Besides, his clown doesn't have green hair."

"Yes, but maybe he knows other clowns who do."

CHAPTER FORTY

A Visit to Information Central

Eric J. Littleton considered himself Information Central when it came to the business of live entertainment – circus performers, musical reviews, burlesque, magic acts, puppet shows, comedy clubs, and the like. Not that he was a gossip; the man simply kept his ear close to the ground.

Having been in the business for nearly half a century, he knew everybody and everybody knew him. He was the go-to guy for a quick booking, replacement, or fill-in. His clients were not A-listers. They would be lucky to be considered B or C.

Based in Chicago, Littleton & Co. covered the Midwest and Southeast. His clients tended to be performers on the way down, not up. Clowns had been a specialty, but circuses were not considered a growth industry.

Bookings being a little slow, the company had been downsized, just him and his secretary remaining. Estelle had been with him longer than his wife (and Eric and Cynthia had just celebrated their ruby wedding anniversary).

Since Littleton & Co.'s phone wasn't exactly ringing off the hook, he welcomed the company when the three women dropped in unannounced that Friday morning.

"We have some questions about your clowns," said Lizzie. "It's about the death of Barffy the Red-Nosed Clown."

"Happy to help."

"We'd like to talk with a few of them," smiled Cookie.

"Yes, can you tell us how to reach them? Maybe give us their addresses?" added Bootsie.

Eric Littleton nodded. "Addresses? No problem." He turned to his old-fashioned Rolodex. "Got 'em right here."

~ ~ ~

Billy Tuckman was taken aback by the chubby woman he found waiting in the lobby of his apartment building, a run-down five-story edifice just a block or two off Miracle Mile. "You've been waiting for me?" he repeated her statement.

"Yes," Bootsie nodded. "You met the other day with Det. Harry Teague. I have a follow-up question."

"How do you know about my talking with that detective?" His facial tics were having a heyday.

"Sorry, I meant to introduce myself. I'm a special assistant to Police Chief Jim Purdue, Harry's boss down in Caruthers Corners." It was only a slight exaggeration.

"Okay, okay. What's your question? It's been a hard day – I played a seven-year-old kid's birthday party – and I'm rather eager to soak my bones in a hot bath. I hate kids."

"Simply, do you have an alibi for the hour before Barffy the Red-Nosed Clown dropped dead?"

"Oh, you think I'm the green-haired clown that threatened that old lady?"

"Convince me you're not."

"Ask any of my troupe. We were there together in the sidelines – all twelve of us – prior to Barffy's demise."

"Thank you, I will."

~ ~ ~

Bootsie had barely got to her car when Lizzie called her iPhone. "Gary Griffin says all the clown car clowns were together before Barffy's death. That your guy can give him an alibi."

Bootsie replied, "And my guy says that your guy can give *him* an alibi."

"Do you think they're covering for each other?"

"If they are, it's a pretty big collusion. I talked with three other members of the clown car troupe. They all say the same thing."

"Hm, in that case, I think we can scratch them off the list."

"Yes. We may as well meet up with Cookie. Wonder if she's had any luck?"

~ ~ ~

"Struck out," reported Cookie. "Topsy wasn't home. Turns out, he's been in jail for the past two weeks. Serving time for a DUI. That's a pretty solid alibi."

"Wonder why Littleton didn't know he was in jail?"

"Kyle Brownell didn't tell him. Afraid Littleton & Co, would drop him as a client if ol' Eric found out. Seems Topsy has a history of drinking. Says he's on thin ice with the booking agent. Asked me not to mention his infraction."

Lizzie sighed. "Let's hope Maddy's having better luck than we did."

~ ~ ~

"Green-haired clowns? Sure, I know a few," said Freddie Madison. He and his men were rolling up hoses in front of the Fire Department when Maddy dropped by for a chat.

"I was hoping you would," said his mother. "I figured with your side career as Sparkplug the Fire Prevention Clown you might know a few other clowns."

"Not as many as you might think. I've never traveled with a circus or done more than regional performances."

"I just need to find one."

"The right one," he corrected. Protective of his fellow clowns. They formed a tight-knit community, as it happens.

"Well, of course," she huffed. Mildly insulted by the implied aspersion.

Freddie continued rolling up a thick fire hose with the help of Willie Sutton, one of the full-time firemen. "There's a clown known as Clover Leaf; he has green hair. Works children's parties down in Indy. Then there's a guy who goes by the handle of Pepper Pot. He works with a small traveling circus out of Ohio. Rumbling Bros. I think it's called, not to be confused with Ringling Bros."

"That's all?" None of those sounded right. They had no connection to the Crazy Carnival.

"Oh, Sprinkles. I guess you could include him."

"Sprinkles?'

"That's the clown Bobby Ray Purdue used to play when he was with the Haney Bros. Circus. As you'll recall, that was back in his 'Lost Boys' days."

Maddy brushed back her silver locks. "That's right, he was a clown before he came home and claimed those riches, became a big philanthropist."

Her son smiled. "He owes all that wealth to the Quilters Club. You guys helped uncover those Watermelon dollars in that family quilt. Who would've thought those old bills would have been worth so much money to collectors."

"Sprinkles, huh?" Maddy repeated thoughtfully. "That's right. I've seen him perform with you on Saturdays. I'd forgotten his clown has green hair."

"Green hair and blue nose and yellow skin speckled with red dots – Sprinkles."

~ ~ ~

Late that afternoon, back at the Quilting Museum, the quartet shared their findings. Lizzie, Bootsie, and Cookie had struck out in searching for the green-haired clown who had left Barffy a threatening message. Despite their pretending otherwise, they were a little irked by Maddy's apparent success.

"Add one more to the list – Bobby Ray Purdue," confirmed their friend.

"My cousin?" exclaimed Bootsie.

"One and the same. We were forgetting his Sprinkles the Clown."

"That's true," admitted Cookie. "But he wasn't on the program at Crazy Carnival." Her usual refrain.

"But his clown has green hair," said Bootsie.

Cookie wasn't convinced. "What does that matter if he wasn't there?"

"We need to double-check that."

"I think we're going to need to prove that – and more – before we accuse Bobby Ray," said Lizzie. Her brow was wrinkled in a frown. "He's one of the town's biggest benefactors."

"Yes," nodded Cookie. "No need to shake that tree without proof he was even at the carnival."

CHAPTER FORTY-ONE

Clown Show

Freddie Madison still made Saturday appearances as Sparkplug the Fire Prevention Clown at the Haney Bros. Zoo & Exotic Animal Refuge, riding around on his little electric firetruck. Sometimes Bobby Ray Purdue joined him, reprising his role as Sprinkles, the clown he'd played when he was a "Lost Boy," and Haney Bros. was a traveling circus.

Kids loved the clowns, the two of them yucking it up and squirting seltzer at each other. Even though Bobby Ray was now a wealthy philanthropist, he maintained a childlike zest for life. That was reflected in his collections – a Fokker biplane, a military tank, a 30-foot dinosaur skeleton, a humongous comic book library, a playground in his backyard – as well as his clowning around.

That's why he'd decided to crash the party at the Caruthers Corners Crazy Carnival with a surprise appearance as Sprinkles. Even Freddie didn't know about these plans.

Barffy's success irked him. He'd had a long-standing feud with that red-nosed idiot, animosity that went back to his days with the circus.

Years ago, Sprinkles and Barffy had appeared on the same program, a county fair in some goshforsaken Midwestern town. Barffy, the big star, had treated Bobby Ray like a dirt-beneath-his-feet peon, ordering him about, belittling him, embarrassing him in front of the crowds. Ever since, he'd held a grudge. Bobby Ray was not one to forget a slight.

When Bobby Ray – after he became rich – founded the Home for Retired Circus Performers, he vowed there would never be a room for Walter Ambrose Bradford. The jerk could go wanting in his old age.

He was disappointed to hear of Barffy's continuing success, becoming a headliner with Ringling Bros. He thought about buying the circus just so he could put Walt Bradford out of work.

But when Barffy dropped dead, he didn't have to worry about that. As that old T-shirt saying proclaimed:

"Outliving your enemy is the best revenge!"

~ ~ ~

Sissy rode her bike over to the Madison house, taking the shortcut. She'd been invited for dinner, the main course being pot roast, one of her favorites. To announce her arrival, she honked her horn. It was one of those silvery trumpets with a squeeze bulb, the device mounted to the handle bars.

Umph-a! Umph-a!

"Sissy, you'll disturb the whole neighborhood," called Maddy from the window. "Why don't you get one of those bells instead of that foghorn. Bells make a less obtrusive sound."

Umph-a! she gave the rubber bulb one more squeeze.

"Sorry," she said impishly. Planting her kickstand in the grass of the front yard.

"Come on in. Dinner's on the table. We have watermelon upside-down cake for dessert. To celebrate your getting your quilt back."

~ ~ ~

The Quilters Club's investigation of the clown's death had come to a stop. If they couldn't question Bobby Ray, they had run out of suspects. Nobody really thought the former "Lost Boy" had anything to do with Barffy's death – what was the motive? – but without a string to unravel, the mystery remained a tight ball of thread.

Maddy hated it when that happened. Usually, their digging up clues went forward, one leading to the next. But here they were stymied.

Be patient, she told herself. Something will turn up. It always did. Crime was messy, leaving loose ends to be found if one looked hard enough.

She just had to wait.

~ ~ ~

As an experienced detective, Harry Teague knew that the longer a case dragged out, the less likely it would be solved. This Barffy the Clown investigation was taking much too long. Several weeks had passed since the opening night of the Crazy Carnival.

So far, they had determined Barffy had been poisoned, but had no clue who did it. That theory about a green-haired clown being responsible seemed to have hit a dead end.

By his count, they had run out of suspects. All the green-haired clowns had provided air-tight alibies. Even Chief Purdue was throwing up his hands.

The Quilters Club had been quiet lately. Had they given up too? The Chief's wife wasn't talking. And that was very unusual for her.

Harry's wife – Penny Heath, crime writer at the *Gazette* – kept pestering him for some inside information. Unfortunately, he had none to give. Today's newspaper's headline had read:

Killer Clown Case Grinds to Halt

Exclusive by Penelope Heath, Crime Reporter

The Caruthers Corners Police has determined that Walter Ambrose Bradford, better known as Barffy the Red-Nosed Clown, was poisoned using a rare toxin called ricin. However, the list of suspects has dwindled as alibies have been checked, leaving the investigation with nowhere to go.

Police Chief James Purdue had no comment.

Caruthers Corners Mayor Mark Tidemore confirmed that the Crazy Carnival will be revived sometimes next year. He called the clown's death "an unfortunate aberration."

Col. Oscar Owensby, manager of Walter Bradford, said Barffy the Red-Nosed Clown had been a "national treasure" and would go down in circus annals alongside Emmett Kelly, Oleg Popov, and Bozo.

Sources close to the Caruthers Corners Police Department say the Killer Clown Case may remain unsolved.

Harry was thankful his wife didn't name him in the article. Nevertheless, he would be the first one his boss suspected of being the leak.

CHAPTER FORTY-TWO

Couples Night

Cozy Café remained open on Sunday nights, serving a special dinner. Two for the price of one. Maisie called it "Couples Night."

She had been surprised to see Bobby Ray Purdue and his girlfriend *du jour* there for dinner. First, since he was one of the richest people in the county, he tended to dine at fancy restaurants in Burpyville or Indy. The Cozy Café was a little beneath him. And second, a man of Bobby Ray's wealth didn't need to take advantage of BOGO dinner specials.

That's why Maisie had paid extra special attention to Bobby Ray's table. What was going on here?

She didn't recognize his date. The stunning blonde could have been a supermodel by the looks of her. And when you had Bobby Ray's kind of money, that was a distinct possibility.

Wealth was an aphrodisiac. Maisie herself had noticed men paying more attention to her since she got her big Hoople inheritance. But they were mostly Casper Milquetoast kinds of guys looking for a free meal ticket. Too bad somebody like Fabio didn't knock on her door.

Bobby Ray must have been trying to charm the blonde. He was talking about his adventures with the circus during his Lost Boys years. He was telling her about founding the exotic animal refuge and the Home for Retired Circus

Performers and how he sometimes reprised his Sprinkles the Clown role for kids on Saturday mornings at Haney Bros. zoo.

"Did you go to the Crazy Carnival?" his date asked. Probably working the conversation around to the dead clown. That had been all anybody wanted to talk about this week.

"I stopped by. But it closed down the minute ol' Barffy bit the dust."

"They say it was a heart attack ..."

"Who knows? I never liked that jerk. I'd dressed up in my Sprinkles costume, planning to crash his act, but my timing was a bit off. He dropped dead before I got the chance."

"So you left?"

"Yeah, but not before I wrote a message on his mirror. A eulogy, as it were. Sent him off with my two cents."

"Two cents? Silly boy, everybody says you're worth millions."

"Give or take," he smiled modestly.

~ ~ ~

The Quilters Club was surprised when Maisie Walters showed up for their Tuesday afternoon meeting. They had just started work on the duplicate Crazy Carnival Pictorial Quilt, the one for the Heglers. Turns out, the couple celebrated their "anniversary" on the date Mary Alice learned she was pregnant, not when Dorothy was conceived.

The tableau was one of activity: Bootsie sorting scraps. Maddy and Cookie clearing off the worktable, packing away remnants of their still-in-progress Crazy Quilts. Lizzie supervising the process. After all, this was her domain, the Hoople Quilting Heritage Museum.

"Hi, Sis," Maddy greeted their visitor. "What brings you here? Want to help us sew a quilt?"

"Not today. Thought I'd pass along a tidbit I heard at dinner Sunday night. At first I wasn't going to mention it. Probably nothing, but the more I thought about it, the more I wondered."

"Juicy gossip?" inquired Lizzie. Always ready for a hot scoop.

"Not exactly. Bobby Ray had dinner with a lady friend Sunday night at the café. I just, uh, happened to overhear part of the conversation. According to Bobby Ray, he went to the opening night of the carnival dressed as Sprinkles the Clown."

"That's interesting," said Bootsie. "We had just added him to our list of Persons of Interest."

"Really?"

"Well, kinda. We were proceeding cautiously."

"Bobby Ray is one of the town's most upstanding citizens," affirmed Lizzie. "You don't accuse a guy like that without lots of evidence."

"He's such a nice guy," nodded Cookie.

"He was a little snot when he was a kid," said Bootsie, rolling her eyes. "He's Jim's cousin, you'll remember."

"True, but he's grown up now – and richer than Croesus," Cookie pointed out.

"He still acts like a kid – all those motorcycles and toys he owns."

"He's a collector."

Bootsie said, "He doesn't collect stamps or coins like a grownup. He has zillions of comic books and trading cards."

"And a dinosaur skeleton and a military tank and a stuffed elephant."

"I don't approve of the stuffed elephant," said Bootsie, the animal lover. "Or that Kodiak bear."

"Nonetheless, we have to treat Bobby Ray carefully," Cookie pointed out. "Like Lizzie said, we need solid evidence."

"What more do you need," huffed Maisie. "I heard him tell that blonde bimbo he was the one who wrote on that clown's mirror. Straight from the horse's mouth."

Maddy sighed. "Hate to insult Bobby Ray, but we'd better go ask him exactly where he was when ol' Barffy dropped dead."

CHAPTER FORTY-THREE

More About Maddy

Madelyn Agnes Taylor Hoople Madison was born in Caruthers Corners, a Hoosier from the top of her silver hair to the tips of her pink toenails. Maddy traced her lineage to the early settlers of the little Indiana town, the Taylors – until she discovered that she had been adopted. That was a shocker. Not to mention that she discovered she had a separated-at-birth fraternal twin. And that they had been the love children of Herbert Hoople, one of the world-famous Hoople Quadruplets.

The Hoople quads used to be a big deal. They once appeared on the cover of *Time* Magazine. Cars and clothing lines had been named after them. They made paid public appearances, did cameos in movies, were featured in national advertising campaigns. Along the way the foursome amassed a huge fortune that had found its way down the family tree to Maddy and Maisie.

However, it was Maddy's husband Beau who was a true descendent of one of the town's Founding Fathers, a lanky pioneer by the name of Col. Beauregard Hollingsworth Madison. That cemented her stature among the local elite. Caruthers Corners took its history very seriously.

Even though Maddy was now quite wealthy, thanks to the Hoople inheritance, she proceeded with her day-to-day life as if she were an ordinary midwestern housewife, a good civic citizen, a devoted grandmother, a member of a sewing bee. The only aberration was the avocation as a crime stopper.

Maddy Madison was a pleasant-looking woman in her mid 60s, blue eyes, ready smile – a double for Ellen Burstyn, the actress in *Alice Doesn't Live Here Anymore* and *Divine Secrets of the Ya-Ya Sisterhood.*

As for her new-found money, it was safely tucked away in a foundation overseen by Barnabas Soltairé, Esq., former manager of the Hoople Quadruplets Trust Fund. She never touched it, except for setting up trust funds for her children and grandchildren. The principle went to philanthropic causes of her choosing, mostly local projects and good deeds.

She often found herself competing with Bobby Ray Purdue in her generosity. Her donations were more strategic; his more impulsive. She supported projects like the Hoople Senior Living Home; he was behind the Retirement Home for Retired Circus Performers. Both worthy causes.

Bobby Ray (and his brother N.L.) were first cousins of Police Chief James Dean Purdue. Jim represented the poor side of the family.

Jim's wife Bootsie resented their "impoverished" public servant status. All her fellow Quilters Club pals were well-to-do: Maddy, with her Hoople inheritance. Lizzie, heir to the Bergamachi banking fortune. Cookie, married to the largest land owner in the county.

Maddy had a secret plan to help equalize this financial imbalance. Jim Purdue was nearing his second attempt at retirement. Why not set up a fat retirement package for the outgoing law officer?

~ ~ ~

Buck Jackson was taken aback by the news. He'd just received word that his daughter – Cecelia's mom – was being released from a rehab center in Birmingham. He was being notified as her next of kin.

What to do?

Should he reach out to her? Or leave her on her own?

Yes, she was his flesh and blood. But she had caused him so much heartache over the years. And her abandonment of her daughter was almost unforgiveable.

Not that he didn't consider the last few years of having Cecilia live with him a blessing. Happiest years of his life. The girl was amazing. Smart, talented, a great singing voice. And all-but-engaged to that nice Madison boy.

What to do?"

Guess he and Sissy needed to have a family meeting.

CHAPTER FORTY-FOUR

Sprinkles the Clown

"Yeah, I was at the carnival dressed as Sprinkles the Clown," admitted Bobby Ray. "What's the big deal?"

"We're curious what you were doing there in costume?" said Maddy. "You weren't part of the show."

"Just a stupid lark," he shrugged. "I was going to crash Freddie's act. He and I do that, being pals. Sometimes I get dressed up as Sprinkles and show up unannounced at the Saturday matinees at Haney Bros. Zoo & Exotic Animal Refuge. He doesn't mind when I join in."

"You know this looks bad. Chief Purdue's theory is that the person who left that threatening message in the dressing room was the one who poisoned Barffy."

"Don't be silly. Cousin Jim knows I'm not a murderer."

"Maybe, maybe not. He doesn't have any other suspects than the person who left that threat."

"Wasn't me. I admit I was there in Clown Alley wearing my Sprinkles outfit. But I was never in Barffy's dressing room."

"Birdie Longstreet saw you there."

"I bumped into Birdie, but it was outside the tent. She said she was looking for the restroom."

"Then what happened?"

"She mistook me for Barffy and started pestering me for an autograph. I told her to leave me alone."

"Birdie said you threatened to cut her throat."

"Did not. That old biddy gets everything wrong. Last month she was claiming that she spotted John F. Kennedy at the retirement home."

"That was Herman Higgins. He *does* look a bit like the late president. Well, without the head wound."

"What I said to Birdie was "Leave me alone or you're gonna get my goat."

"You don't have a goat."

"Aw c'mon, Maddy. You know the old expression. It's not exactly a death threat."

~ ~ ~

"He admitted it?" said Lizzie.

"Not exactly. He admits to being there in Clown Alley, but denies having anything to do with Barffy's death."

"What about threatening Birdie?"

"Yes, he said he would cut her throat," Bootsie nodded.

"Claims she misheard him. That he said her pestering him for an autograph was about to 'get his goat.'"

"'Get his goat?'" repeated Lizzie, red hair flashing in the sun streaming down from the skylight. They were gathered there in the crafts room at the Quilting Museum. "What's that mean?"

Cookie delved into her memory banks. "The phrase 'to get someone's goat' comes from the French expression *prendre la chevre*, which means 'to take the goat.' Naturally, taking someone's goat would anger its owner. The phrase means to irritate someone."

"Why would her asking for an autograph irk him?"

"Because she thought he was Barffy."

"That would do it," laughed Bootsie. She knew her husband's cousin was pretty thin skinned.

"I wouldn't be surprised if Birdie misheard him," said Maddy. "Not only is she ditzy, but she's hard of hearing too. The other day I greeted her, 'How do you do?' She thought I said I'd seen a caribou."

"Aren't those reindeers?"

"Kinda," said Bootsie. "They mostly live in the arctic, I believe."

" 'The North American range of caribou extends from Alaska through the Yukon, the Northwest Territories and Nunavut throughout the tundra ... south through the Canadian Rocky Mountains,' " said Cookie, quoting from some obscure tome called *Mammals of Canada.*

"Huh?" said Lizzie. Geography wasn't her strongpoint.

"I think she's saying there are no caribou near here," translated Maddy, trying to suppress a smile.

"We'd better report this to my hubby," said Bootsie. "We promised to keep him fully informed."

"What do we have to report?" grumbled Lizzie. "The migration range of caribou?"

"No," said Bootsie. "That Bobby Ray Purdue has confessed to being at the murder scene. And that he was wearing a clown costume and a wig with green hair."

CHAPTER FORTY-FIVE

Oxymoron

Police Chief Jim Purdue didn't seem pleased with this news that his cousin was now on the suspect list. Not only was Bobby Ray one of the richest guys in town, he was a public benefactor bestowing money on numerous worthy causes – in particular the Home for Retired Circus Performers. You couldn't just go around accusing a guy like that of being a killer clown.

This was like a nightmare, he told himself. Sometimes he hated his job.

"Killer Clown," joked Cookie. "Isn't that an oxymoron? Like Army Intelligence? Or Jumbo Shrimp?" She liked wordplay – puns, oxymorons, palindromes. Even *The New York Times* crossword.

Jim Purdue scowled. "Kinda like Police Chief. I think that's a contradiction in terms. I don't feel like I'm in charge, with you busybodies sticking your noses in my murder investigation."

"But we're only helping out, dear," inveigled his pudgy wife.

"Right," said Maddy. "You were looking for a green-haired clown ... and we found him for you."

"Yeah, but this isn't the solution I want."

"What were you expecting?" interjected Lizzie. "Col. Mustard in the Library with a Lead Pipe."

"Anybody but Bobby Ray Purdue. I can't arrest him."

"You can if he's guilty," insisted Maddy. With her son-in-law being a former big-league lawyer, she had a strong sense of crime and punishment.

"But he *can't* be guilty."

"*Humph.* You just don't want him to be guilty," said Bootsie. "He's the best suspect you have."

"You're saying he murdered Barffy the Red-Nosed Clown with a rare poison called ricin? Where would he get that?" argued the Police Chief.

Maddy squinted her eyes at Jim. "Bobby Ray is rich. If anyone hereabout could afford to buy a rare poison on the black market, it's your cousin."

"That's not proof. You're rich, Maddy. You could afford to buy ricin too."

"But I'm not a green-haired clown. And I've got no grudge against Walter Ambrose Bradford."

"True. But *some*body fits that bill."

"Bobby Ray," offered Bootsie. "Case closed."

"You never did like that side of my family," complained her husband.

"The rich side? He and his brother N.L. have never done anything for us."

"That's not the point. We need somebody – other than Bobby Ray – who wanted to see Barffy dead."

"We know Barffy was killed with ricin," mused Maddy. "The second toxicology report confirmed that. But how was it administered? Maybe if we can figure out that, it will give us a clue who did it."

Chief Purdue sighed. "Maybe we oughta talk with Doc Medford about that."

CHAPTER FORTY-SIX

The Poison

Dr. Franklin Delano Medford disliked having his work questioned by these Nosy Parkers almost as much as Chief Purdue did. The Quilters Club as usual was stepping on toes. Only their success rate kept critics at bay. That, and Maddy's son-in-law – the town's mayor. He had asked Doc and Jim to cooperate.

"Look here, ladies," Doc Medford huffed, pushing his rimless glasses onto the bridge of his nose. "I can't prove how the poison was administered. But I can tell you how it wasn't."

"I don't follow you," said Lizzie.

"Me neither," said Bootsie.

"Perhaps you'd best explain that statement," said Maddy. Lizzie nodded.

Jim Purdue stood in the background near the door to Doc's medical office, saying nothing. He didn't look happy. Harry Teague parked himself next to his boss, eager to hear Doc Medford's theories. The case needed a breakthrough.

"I can tell you the ricin wasn't injected. I went over every inch of his body with a magnifying glass looking for any needle tracks. Nary pinprick on his body. I even looked between his toes and inside his mouth."

"Okay," nodded Maddy, coming to better understand what he'd been saying.

"Also, he didn't ingest it. We – me and the state technicians – examined his stomach contents. Even bowel samples. No sign of ricin."

"That will be a big relief to Maisie," muttered Chief Purdue. "She was afraid it was something he ate at Cozy Café."

"She can quit worrying about that," said the coroner. "His tenderloin cutlet was there, but nothing else."

"What does that leave?" asked Lizzie.

"Inhalation," said the coroner. "But I can't prove much there. There's some inflammation of the nasal passage, but we have no idea how he breathed it in. Did someone spray it in a seltzer bottle? Put it in a nasal inhaler? Turn it into a gas – if that can even be done?"

"Any sign Barffy had allergies or asthma?" asked Cookie. Focusing on the inhaler theory.

Doc Medford turned up his palms, as if to show they were empty. "None, according to his medical records. We pulled them from his primary care doctor in Chicago."

"We looked into those seltzer bottles the clowns were spraying everybody with," said the Police Chief. "No trace of ricin in them. And nobody they squirted got sick and died."

"And we didn't turn up any inhalers," noted Harry Teague.

"So we're stumped," Jim Purdue concluded with a sigh.

"No, we're not," said Maddy. Snapping her fingers as the idea came to her. "I know how it was done."

"Huh?" said the coroner, caught off-guard. "You do?"

"It's as plain as the nose on your face."

"How's that?"

"Barffy's big red nose," she said. "Someone put ricin in it. When Barffy got into costume, he clamped that big red proboscis on his nose and breathed it in as he went about his act."

"I'll be darned," said Doc Medford. "That would explain why he strangled and grabbed his throat, rather than his chest like you might with a heart attack."

"Exactly," said Cookie. "Inhaled ricin provides symptoms such as respiratory distress, fever, cough, and nausea. Heavy sweating may follow as fluid builds up in the lungs (pulmonary edema). Breathing becomes even more difficult, and the skin might turn blue."

"Death from ricin poisoning could take place within 24 to 36 hours of exposure," nodded the coroner. "But timing depends on the amount administered. A rubber nose packed with the deadly powder would take much less time, allowing him to nearly finish his act before collapsing."

"All that's very interesting," Jim Purdue allowed. "But we still have to figure out who put the poison in Barffy's big red nose."

~ ~ ~

After the revelations at Doc Medford's office, the Quilters Club's returned to Maddy's big Victorian house on Melon Pickers Row to compare notes. Maddy's grandson and his girlfriend were there waiting for them. As junior members of the Quilters Club, they didn't want to be left out.

Turns out, the Dearborn Observatory remained closed due to a chip detected in the refracting lens, so N'yen got a few extra days off. He took the opportunity to head back to Caruthers Corners – and Sissy.

Maddy shared her new theory with them.

"Very clever," the boy said, "putting the poison powder in the clown's rubber nose. How did you figure it out?"

"Sissy's bicycle horn. I remembered seeing her squeezing that big rubber bulb to make it honk. Reminded me it was hollow."

"Way cool," grinned the girl.

"Doc Medford hadn't checked the nose till now," nodded Bootsie. "Plenty of ricin powder still in there."

"Good so far," said Cookie. "Now all we have to do is figure out who did it."

"Are we back to the green-haired clown?" asked Lizzie.

"I dunno," hesitated Maddy. "Any ideas?"

"Forget the clown angle," suggested N'yen. "We need to figure out who had access to Barffy's costume before the performance – clown or not. Who had an opportunity to put the poison in Barffy rubber nose."

"That could be a long list," Cookie warned. "There are always plenty of people buzzing about during a circus performance."

"We can eliminate the clowns anyway," said Lizzie. "All twelve of those clown car cronies alibi each other."

"And no one believes Freddie or Bobby Ray were involved," Maddy added. Getting that on the record.

"Who else then?" asked Sissy. Her face was scrunched up like a little raisin.

"Let's go through the list," said N'yen. "Everybody who was inside the Big Top tent before the show started."

"Even the audience members?" exclaimed Bootsie. "That's impossible."

"For now, we'll ignore them. Stick to people connected to the carnival." The boy was taking charge. How quickly they grow up, thought Maddy proudly.

"Where do we start?" asked Lizzie. She plopped down in a comfortable wingback chair, ready to get to work.

"Mark was there, of course, acting as ringmaster. But I think we can eliminate him," said Maddy. After all, he was not only the mayor, he was married to her daughter Tilly. Everyone knew he was a man of integrity.

"How about the other performers?" said Bootsie. She sprawled on the couch, taking up most of the space. Getting comfortable for a long haul. This was going to take some time.

Cookie easily ticked them off. "Aside from the clowns, we had the Flying Floyds; a group of juggling unicyclists; and Swami Bombay with Happy the Elephant."

"What about circus workers – what do they call them?" asked Sissy.

"Roustabouts," supplied Lizzie.

"That's a funny word."

"The word comes from 'roust,' which is an alteration of 'rouse,' a verb from Middle English that originally meant 'to shake the feathers' – as in the way a bird might ruffle its feathers or shake its plumage when it is settling down or grooming itself," explained Cookie. "It means an unskilled or casual laborer."

"Thank you, Ms. Smarty Pants," said Bootsie. That memory thing was downright irritating at times. The police chief's wife could barely remember where she put her car keys.

"Mark or Beau will have a list of everybody hired to raise the tent or run the electricity cables and such," Maddy assured them.

"What about the food people?" said Bootsie. The plump housewife was always thinking about eating. "You know, hot dog vendors, cotton candy spinners, popcorn sellers."

"If you're going to include everybody," said N'yen, "what about all those sideshow freaks. One of them could have wandered over."

"You shouldn't call them freaks," corrected his girlfriend. "To them, that's like using the N-word."

"I thought it was called a Freak Show," the boy protested.

"In the old days," Maddy allowed. "But most of those physically challenged people you're talking about are our neighbors from up in Crackleton Crossing."

"Neighbors?" snorted Lizzie. "They are *your* relatives."

True, it had been proven that Maddy and her twin sister Maisie were descended from Granny Crackleton, the matriarch of that den of thieves, deranged personalities, and congenitally disadvantaged ... well, freaks. That family was so inbred that the Baltimore Geographic Society had spent a year documenting their infirmities and intertwined family lines, then published a three-inch-thick book about it. Maddy didn't like to talk about it, fearful of what DNA might be floating around in her genes. She couldn't help but think of the truth in that Steven Wright joke: The problem with the gene pool is that there is no lifeguard.

"So they are," she responded to Lizzie's smart-mouth comment. "We don't get to pick our relatives."

"I was just kidding, Hon."

"No offense taken."

"A lot of the Crackletons turned out for the sideshow," Bootsie told them. "The deal was they got to keep all their own sideshow ticket money."

"I saw the roster," affirmed Cookie, ticking off the names from memory. "The participants included Jebediah Crackleton, his son Dub, Phil Jinks, Chewy Johnson, and her daughter Babs. Randolph Johnson and his resorbed brother Rex were the sideshow's headliners."

"Hold the front door," said Lizzie. "I thought Jebediah and Dub were still in prison." Jeb was a 7-foot-tall giant; his son Dub was a dwarf. They had been busted for running a loan shark business out of the family's convenience store.

"Jeb and Dub were released last year," Bootsie reminded them. "They're still on parole."

"What about Granny Crackleton?" asked Cookie.

"She's ailing," said Maddy. "On her last legs, as they say."

"And her brother Ed?"

"Ed Crackleton was there working the crowd," said Bootsie with the authority of a police chief's wife. "As you know, Ed manages a team of pickpockets, purse snatchers, and grifters – all family members."

"How does he get away with that?" Lizzie wanted to know. She'd had her purse snatched just last month. It had been one of her favorites, a genuine Dior.

"Everybody's aware of Ed's gang, but nobody can prove anything," sighed Bootsie. "Arrest one pickpocket, Ed just sends out another."

"We'll never get through this list," complained Maddy. "Too many people could have walked into Barffy's dressing room and poured that poison powder into his big rubber nose."

"True. We'll have to divide and conquer," decided N'yen. "Otherwise we'll never get through the list."

"How do we do that, Mr. Brainiac?" said Lizzie.

"Each of us talk with someone who can give us the scoop on a particular group. The Crackletons, the performers, the roustabouts, and such."

"Like who?"

"Grammy can go talk with Granny Crackleton. That ol' witch will know if any of her clan was involved in that clown's death."

Lizzie wasn't convinced. "Why would she rat on one of her children or grandchildren?"

N'yen had the answer. "To avoid the police coming down on the whole community. She knows they can't withstand close scrutiny with all their illegal activities."

"Okay," replied Sissy. "What about those roustabouts?"

"There was a boss who oversaw them."

"That would be George Wilkerson, the Caruthers Corners' Director of Public Works," said Lizzie. "He volunteered."

"Right," said Bootsie. "George is close to his crews. He will know who are the shifty ones, hot heads who might be dangerous. That will narrow down who we need to talk with."

Lizzie nodded. "George goes hunting with my husband."

"Then you tackle him," suggested N'yen.

"Uh, all right."

"And how about all the other performers?" asked Cookie. "You know, the jugglers and trapeze artists."

"Why don't you go talk with Swami Bombay? He can glean information from the performers, being one of them."

"Good idea," she nodded. "I'll do that."

Juan Martinez (stage name Swami Bombay) managed the Haney Bros. Zoo & Exotic Animal Refuge. A former mentalist, lion tamer, and strong man, he handled Happy the Elephant. He was very loyal to Cookie's husband Ben, who had donated the land for the animal refuge. He would help them as a favor to Ben.

"I'll talk to the food vendors," volunteered Bootie. A little too willingly perhaps. "Most of them are local housewives who set up the food booths. I know them all."

"What about those carny folk with Anderson Amusements?" Lizzie reminded them. "Y'know, those guys who ran the Tilt-A-Whirl, the Merry-Go-Round, the Bumper Cars."

"Why don't you talk with Mac Braselton," suggested Cookie. Mac was a town employee, the guy who operated the

Ferris Wheel on the far side of the Town Square. "He used to work with Anderson Amusements. He'll know if anything hinky was going on with the ride operators."

"Talk with *both* George Wilkerson and Mac Braselton?"

"You can do it," said Maddy. "You're a charmer."

Lizzie seemed to puff up like a preening hen. "I *am*, aren't I?"

"Sissy and I will call Barffy's manager, see what he has to say," said N'yen.

"I've already talked with Col. Owensby" said Maddy. "But I guess it won't hurt to talk with him again."

"Well, I think that covers everybody," N'yen concluded. He brushed his hair out of his eyes. He was growing it rather long lately. College culture taking hold.

"That's a good plan," smiled Sissy, admiringly.

"May not work," shrugged the Asian boy. "Nobody's going to admit to murder. But it may eliminate some people – and turn up some hints of where to look next."

"What are we looking for?" asked Lizzie.

"*Cui bono,*" he said.

CHAPTER FORTY-SEVEN

The Second Debate

The podium in front of Town Hall again had been erected overnight. Microphones were in place for this second debate between Mayor Mark Tidemore and his opponent Ken Wurgler. Fewer people had turned out this time; but the press was dutifully on hand.

Lucius Plancus was again at the front, ready to ask questions. He'd spent hours crafting some zingers, designed to play the Gotcha Game. Tripping up politicians was good for ratings. WZUR could us a little boost.

This time, Ken had insisted the Mayor go first. That way he could contradict any points that came up in Mark Tidemore's speech. Forget about his platform of protecting jobs; he would oppose whatever the mayor said. If Mark said *black*, he'd say *white*.

This time there was no moderator. *Gazette* publisher Justin Nightly had dropped out due to a painful ingrown toenail. No loss. Nobody wanted another Freedom of the Press speech.

"Ken, good to see you," said Mark, shaking his opponent's hand.

"Yes, you too," muttered Ken Wurgler. "Are we ready to start?"

"Sure, why not? I go first this time?"

"Your turn."

"Very well," responded the Mayor, stepping up to his lectern. He was tall and handsome, well dressed in a finely tailored suit, like an advertisement for Abercrombie & Fitch. He tapped the mike with his finger to make sure it was live. After surveying the small crowd, he began with a toothy smile:

"Ladies and gentlemen, citizens of Caruthers Corners. As you know, I am running for mayor again. I'd like to have your vote."

Stopping, Mark took a step back, signaling he was finished.

"Uh, that's all?" asked his opponent.

"That's all. Your turn."

Ken leaned toward his microphone. "Thank you for coming out today." Then he paused, not sure what to say next. There was nothing to rebut. He was frozen, overtaken by a sudden case of stage fright. He simply stared glassy-eyed at the audience.

Lucius Plancas saw this as an opportunity to get a question in. Switching on his recorder, he thrust the mike in Ken Wurgler's direction. "Excuse me, sir," he began, "but can you tell us what you'd do, if elected, that would be different than the current administration?"

"Well, uh, I'd cancel these ill-fated town promotions. We're not a tourist town, so why pretend to be? I for one am sick of all these out-of-towners."

"So you'd do away with the Watermelon Festival?"

"Maybe not that one."

"How about the Shakespeare in the Park?"

"Some culture is good."

"What about a repeat of the Crazy Carnival?" Plancus pressed.

"Perhaps if it were done right, yes."

The newscaster went in for the kill. "So you're saying you'd change nothing. If that's the case, why change mayors?"

"Change is good," the man declared, fumbling to straighten his toupee. It was slipping from all the sweat on his skin. "I am an agent of change."

Plancus swung his mike toward Mayor Tidemore. "Your comment, sir?"

"As my father-in-law Beau Madison likes to say, 'If it ain't broke, don't fix it.' Vote for me and get more of the same."

The small crowd roared their agreement.

"Another term, another term," they began to chant.

~ ~ ~

Ken Wurgler looked it up. There was no term limit for a mayor. Mark Tidemore was likely to hold his position for the next twenty years. Not great prospects for an ambitious man like Ken.

Drat!

ARTICLE II: LEGISLATIVE DEPARTMENT
SECTION 2-3. MAYOR: QUALIFICATIONS, TERM, TERM LIMITS, DUTIES.

The mayor's term of office is four years, with no restrictions on the number of terms that may be served. Mayors must reside within the municipality and do so for at least one year before the election.

The mayor is the chief executive officer of the municipality and is responsible for all operations within each department. Indiana is considered a "strong mayor" state, where the mayor is directly responsible for the business affairs of the city. The mayor appoints each department head and many board and

commission members, and presides over the Town
Council and the Board of Public Works.

The mayor ultimately is responsible for the
enforcement of local ordinances, compliance with state
statutes, signing all bonds, deeds, city contracts as well
as approving or vetoing ordinances and resolutions.

Ken knew the debates hadn't gone well. Nevertheless, he
told himself he would finish his campaign for mayor with
vigor. He still had a few tricks up his sleeve. If N.L. Purdue
would agree to fund it, he'd blitz the town with radio and TV
ads. He'd imprint his face in the mind of every voting citizen
of Caruthers Corners. He'd put up a battle like no one
hereabouts had ever seen. He was determined to win. He
wanted to be mayor, then a state representative, and
eventually Indiana's governor. He had it all planned out.

But if he lost, he knew that would be the end of his
wannabe political career.

CHAPTER FORTY-EIGHT

A New Round of Interviews

Lizzi started off her interviews with McKenzie Braselton. Mac looked like a dustbowl farmer from an old WPA photograph. He wore a rumbled fedora pulled down to his oversized ears, shielding his face from the sun. Jeans and worn plaid shirt completed the look. Running the town's Ferris wheel was an outdoors job, but a good one for a semi-retired amusement rides carny.

The former carny was happy to talk with Lizzie Ridenour, an excuse to shut down the wheel for a brief while. Besides, she was a mighty fine looking woman for her age. He had a thing for skinny redheads.

"Hiya, Mrs. Ridenour. How's the hubby?"

"Out fishing as usual," she replied. Since retiring, the former bank president rarely missed a day fishing on the Wabash. Their freezer was packed with bass and catfish and bluegill.

"Envy him. I like the children, but watching this wheel go round gets old."

"I can imagine."

"What can I do for you, Mrs. Ridenour?"

"Has to do with that clown that died."

"Barffy? I've met him back in the day. Worked some of the same fairs. Can't say I liked him. A most detestable fellow."

"Do you still have ties to your old carny friends?"

"Some."

"Have you heard anything through the grapevine ... any hint that one of them did Barffy in?"

"Nothing like that. Nobody's shedding a tear, but nobody's taking credit for it either. Everybody thought it was a heart attack until word leaked out that he'd been poisoned."

~ ~ ~

George Wilkerson had agreed to oversee the workers who put the Crazy Carnival together. As Director of Public Works, he was used to getting things done. And he had crews at his disposal.

Hiring a few extras as roustabouts, he and his small army of workers had raised the tents, built the concession stands, and rigged the power supply in a matter of days. He had a knack for organization, a natural sense of leadership, and the iron will to make things happen on schedule. He deserved a lot of credit in rebuilding the town's infrastructure following that devastating 2018 tornado. Mayor Mark Tidemore referred to him as "my right-hand, go-to, get-it-done guy."

George's darkly-lit office looked like the den of a big game hunter, mounted trophies covering the walls. A deer, a wild boar, a mountain goat, a bear, even a gazelle from Africa. In addition to hunting, he'd enjoyed the hobby of taxidermy since he was a boy. Some people thought he was kind of weird.

Lizzie had set up a meeting with him following her confab with Mac Braselton. Being one of Edgar's hunting buddies, he'd cleared his calendar to accommodate her. She found his office a little distasteful in that she was against killing animals for sport. Even though her husband was an avid hunter, she refused to allow him to display any of his trophies in their large Tara-like mansion out on River Road.

"Lizzie, my dear. How are you?" George greeted her effusively. Taking her hand, patting it. He kind of fancied himself a Ladies' Man.

"Just fine, George. I'm here on official business," she said, removing her hand.

"Official business?"

"The Quilters Club is looking into that clown's death."

"I'm not sure Chief Purdue would consider you gals official," he said cautiously.

"The Mayor has given us his blessing. And Jim Purdue knows what we're up to."

"Well, let's not quibble. What can I do for you?"

Lizzie leaned closer, almost seductively. "I need to know if any of your carnival workers might have killed Barffy the Red-Nosed Clown."

He leaned back in his padded desk chair, as if distancing himself. "How would I know that?"

"C'mon, George. You have your ear to the ground. I'm betting you have some lieutenants who keep you informed about rumors, maleficences, crimes, bad behavior."

"Yes, you could say that," he fell prey to her flattery. "But I haven't heard anything about that clown's death."

"Can you ask around? Any hint would be helpful."

"Sure, I can do that. But I highly doubt any of my crews would go that far, killing someone. Some of them might have rough edges. Probably could be dangerous under certain circumstances. That said, there's nothing to make me think any of them croaked that clown."

~ ~ ~

Cookie found Swami Bombay feeding the lions. She stood outside the cage, watching as he tossed chucks of bloody red meat to the giant cats. "Got a minute, Juan," she called to the dark-skinned man.

"Sure thing, Miss Cookie. Let me finish handing out these choice cuts. Meat department at the Food Lion saves these for the boys. Food Lion feeding the lions – kinda like a professional courtesy."

She watched as the bigger lion pawed at him, begging for more food. "Isn't that dangerous?"

"Not really. Old Grumpy ain't got no teeth. Lionel over there's the one that'd eat you."

"Good to know."

He stepped out of the cage and secured the door behind him. "Now what's on your mind, Miss Cookie?"

"It's about that dead clown. Guess you've heard it was murder."

"Ben told me it was some kinda poison."

"That's right. A rare toxin that comes from castor oil seeds. Called ricin. You may have heard of it. Those plants are native to India."

"Uh, I'm actually from Mexico," Juan Martinez reminded her.

Her cheeks turned red. "Oh, that's right. I forgot. You play the role of Swami Bombay so well."

"What about that dead clown?"

"The Quilters Club needs your help. We're investigating Walt Bradford's death – that was the clown's real name. Can you help us figure out if any of the circus performers were involved?"

"You want me to be a snitch?"

"No," she said with some irritation, "we want you to be a good citizen. You are an American citizen, aren't you? Or are you still a Mexican?"

He laughed. "I will always be a Mexican. But I got my American citizenship twenty years ago."

"Could one of the performers have poisoned Barffy the Clown?"

"How would I know that?"

"Because you and your elephant were there with all of the other performers, waiting to go on. Did one of them disappear long enough to have planted the poison in Barffy's dressing room. Would have been about an hour or so before he started his act.

"Hm, lemme think. Couldn't have been them fellows with the clown car. They huddled there together the whole time, limbering up so they could pack themselves in that little Fiat."

"You're sure?"

"Wasn't watching them every minute," he said evasively. No need to get sideways with those cantankerous clowns.

"Who else then?" She ticked off the list of circus performers from her flypaper memory – the unicyclists, the Flying Floyds.

"Them one-wheel bicycle fellows, they stuck together too, riding around in circles and practicing their juggling."

"That leaves the aerialists."

"The who?"

"Those trapeze artists – the Flying Floyds."

"Oh, Jon Floyd and his daughter Prissy. Lemme think. As I recall she went to the restroom. And he had to go back to his dressing room to get some chalk for his hands. Them flyers are fussy about their hands. All calloused up from hanging onto the trapeze bars."

"Any other performers I'm overlooking?" she asked. The roster was imprinted on her brain, but maybe there was some unbilled act she didn't know about.

"Others? Just me. But I had to be there with Happy. Can't have an elephant roaming around without a handler."

~ ~ ~

Bootsie liked her assignment. Going from home to home – actually, kitchen to kitchen – to talk with the women who put together the food concessions for the carnival was like being invited to a smorgasbord. She sampled watermelon turnovers at Ethel Kensinger's; fried brie at Lorraine Elwood's; Alice B. Toklas brownies at Brenda Spunger's; homemade taffy at Wanda Schaeffer's; and a large watermelon milkshake at Maisie's diner. She probably gained ten pounds, she told herself. But it was all in the line of duty.

She knew there was little likelihood that any of these local housewives were involved in the death of a from-out-of-town circus performer. Besides, Doc Medford confirmed that the toxic ricin had not been ingested, so the food angle was a dead end. But she enjoyed noshing her way through the community – "eliminating suspects," as she put it.

One clue turned up though: Wanda Schaeffer, who had managed the cotton candy booth, said she saw Three Eyes Johnson sneaking into a tent. She meant to report it but her husband Fat Karl told her to forget it, not get involved.

"You're sure it was Three Eyes?"

"Hard to confuse him with anybody else."

"Excuse me a sec, Wanda. I need to call Maddy Madison right away and tell her about this. By the way, this taffy is delicious."

CHAPTER FORTY-NINE

Maddy's Family Visit

Maddy dreaded her assignment, calling on Sarah Celine "Granny" Crackleton, head of the community known for its miscreants, weirdos, and physical aberrations. Not to mention being Maddy's biological grandmother.

Some people claimed Granny was a witch. Others said she was insane. Still others branded the old hag as a moral degenerate, having copulated with father and brothers alike. Maddy didn't want to know any details. She worried about inherited traits and contaminated gene pools.

Granny lived in a tiny shack at the Crossing, across the street from the family-owned convenience store. Her youngest daughter Faith Ann Ritchie managed the store, on call to deliver Big Red Cola whenever the old woman got a hankering. Everybody catered to Granny Crackleton's biddings.

Maddy found Granny sitting on a daybed on her shady front porch. "What d'you want?" the old woman shouted as Maddy stepped out of her shiny new Buick SUV. "Gonna share some of that Hoople money with your poor ol' grandma?"

"How much do you need?"

"A million dollars. And I'll take a check."

Maddy couldn't help but smile. "What would you do with a million dollars?"

"Buy me a Big Red bottling factory. I dearly love that stuff."

"A business investment?"

"If you wanna call it that."

"Got a question for you: Did any of your kin kill that clown last week?"

"Naw, we Crackletons ain't murderers. Just thieves. Ed's boys did pretty good at that carnival on opening night. Too bad your son-in-law closed it down."

"Somebody got killed."

"A clown – who cares about clowns?"

"The police are going to come up here and interview everybody. You don't want that, do you?"

The old woman screwed up her wrinkled face. "Why would they do that?"

"Because Chief Purdue thinks a Crackleton killed that clown. He's going to turn the place inside out looking for the guilty party. Wouldn't it be better to put a bug in my ear so everybody doesn't get rousted?"

"You want me to sacrifice somebody who didn't do it? I can do that if it keeps the cops away. A reasonable tradeoff." The old woman was nothing if not pragmatic.

"No, we want the guilty party."

"I ain't got 'im."

"What about Randolph Johnson. Somebody saw him sneak into that clown's dressing room. He could have planted the ricin poison."

"Three Eyes? Where would he get a fancy poison? If he did it, he woulda used rat poison or strychnine."

That made sense to Maddy. But she plowed on. "Could I speak with Randolph?"

"Go ahead if you wanna. Him and Rex are over at the convenience store."

CHAPTER FIFTY

Three Eyes

Randolph Johnson was very off-putting in his appearance, what with that third eye in the middle of his forehead. This eye was all that was left of his brother Rex, what doctors called a vanishing twin. People speculated how much of Rex was hidden inside Randolph. Some claimed the third eye could look one way, while the Randolph's two regular orbs were staring off in the other direction. Eerie, to say the least.

Maddy found him sitting at a round wooden table in the back corner of the convenience store with his cousin Jebediah. Ever since getting out of prison, Jeb had resumed his lucrative business as a loan shark, leaving management of the store to his sister Faith Ann and son Dub. The table in back was his "office."

"Randolph, may I speak with you?" Maddy said, stepping up to the large wooden table.

"Uh, I guess so. You're my cousin Madelyn Madison, ain't you?"

Maddy had to swallow hard to acknowledge the relationship. "That's right," she replied, forcing a smile.

Jeb interjected, "What are you doing up here at Crackleton Crossing? A little outta your neighborhood, I'd say."

"I came to speak with Randolph."

"Three Eyes got nothing to say to you."

"Granny said it was all right to talk with him."

"That old woman's half crazy."

"Half?"

"Hey, she's your grandma. What does that make you?"

"She's your mother," Maddy retorted. "What does that make you?"

"A giant," he said. "But looks like you turned out fairly normal."

"So far," she replied. "More than Randolph here."

Three Eyes turned all three irises toward her. "Don't be casting aspersion at me and Rex. We're very comfortable living together."

"Randolph, somebody saw you slipping into a tent at last Friday night's carnival. What were you doing?"

"Just looking about. Rex likes to see things. That's about all he can do."

"So you admit you went into Barffy the Clown's tent?"

"Don't know whose it was. But I did see a clown in there. And an old woman, the one what they call Birdie."

"Three Eyes, shut your mouth," advised his cousin. "Don't say nothing more 'fore we get you a lawyer."

Maddy headed this off. "Randolph, you and Rex don't need a lawyer if you did nothing wrong."

"Didn't do nothing wrong. When I seed that clown and that Birdie woman, I got out of there. Nearly tripped over that other guy."

"What other guy."

The one carrying an apple."

"An apple?"

"Yeah, a red plastic apple."

"Could it have been a clown's nose?"

"You think this guy snatched off the clown's nose. Like in that nursery rhyme about four and twenty blackbirds?"

She leaned closer, putting a hand on his arm. "Did you recognize this man?"

"Sure I did," said Three Eyes Johnson. "He's that fellow who can fly. Do you think he was there to see that bird woman?"

~ ~ ~

"That fellow who could fly," repeated N'yen. "He's gotta mean the head of the Flying Floyds."

"Swami Bombay said Jonathan Floyd went to his dressing room before the show to get some chalk for his hands," Cookie pointed out. "He could have been planting the ricin in Barffy's red rubber nose."

"Where was Barffy at the time?" asked N'yen. "We need to create a timeline."

"Dunno," said Cookie. "Juan didn't say."

"Mark said Barffy didn't come out till the last minute," replied Maddy.

N'yen nodded, his dark hair flopping "His manager – that Col. Owensby – said Walt Bradford always waited to get into his clown suit at the last minute so he wouldn't sweat in it."

"Good info," said Cookie.

"N'yen and me talked with that Chicago booking agent too," added Sissy.

Cookie was surprised. "How did you talk with him?"

Sissy held up her iPhone. "There's this little invention Alexander Graham Bell came up with ..."

"Eric Littleton – we spoke with him too," said Lizzie. "Mostly about Billy Tuckman and those clown car clowns. Did he have anything new to add?"

"Just that Barffy was threatening to retire."

"Not surprising," said Cookie. "He was 72, going on 73."

CHAPTER FIFTY-ONE

Swami Bombay and his Elephant

Happy the Elephant was one of the retired animals from Haney Bros. Circus. Happy was thought to be about 30 years old. Elephants have a lifespan up to 60 or 70 years. The oldest elephant in the world was an Asian elephant named Changalloor Dakshayani who reached 89.

Juan Martinez had been caring for Happy for 22 years, give or take. He'd been working with the circus as a mentalist (i.e. Swami Bombay) when Happy was acquired from Eckert Entertainment & Traveling Show. That was when old Hiram Eckert died and his estate was sold off to satisfy creditors.

In addition to his mind-reading act, Juan had taken on the job of elephant handler. He liked it, quickly bonding with Happy. They were a good pair, working together as if they'd been doing it forever.

Juan would ride around the ring on Happy's back like a potentate. Happy would walk on his hind legs upon command. The elephant had the ability to balance on a large red-and-white ball. He was a very talented pachyderm.

Rival circuses had tried to hire the pair away, but Juan Martinez was loyal to the Haney Bros. and also Happy was their property. This was before they signed all the animals – lions and tiger, and horses – over to the refuge.

Big Bill and Little William were gone now, bless their souls. And Juan was manager of Haney Bros. Zoo & Exotic Animal Refuge. He had a cottage behind the Home for Retired Circus Performers. One bedroom, but with bath and kitchen. That was much better than the accommodations he'd endured when the circus was on the road.

He thought back over the Crazy Carnival's opening night. He and Happy had been standing there on the sidelines, waiting their turn. The Klown Kar Krew had been huddled next to their tricked-out Fiat. And the Flying Floyds had been lined up next to them. The unicyclists – the Juggling Juggernauts, they were called – kept to themselves, practicing across the way, riding in circles.

He remembered the Floyds taking breaks, the girl going off to tinkle, her old man off to chalk his hands. But there was one other guy who'd disappeared for a while, that driver of the clown car. Where had he gone?

He'd forgotten to mention that to Miss Cookie.

Well, he'd leave that up to the police to find out. After talking to the 12 members of the Klown Kar Krew, they were sure to have the answers. Those idiot clowns could never keep a story straight.

~ ~ ~

That night Aggie called her dad to see how his campaign was going. He'd never really had to run a serious one before, never being opposed in his bid for mayor.

"Hi, Sweetie," he greeted her. "What's up?"

"Just aced my history test."

"Good for you. That was a hard course when I was there."

"I'm gonna celebrate by meeting some friends at Mory's after this call."

"For years, women weren't allowed in Mory's."

"Now they're not only allowed in, they can become members. The membership fee is modest for college students but $100 annually for others."

"I love their buttered lobster roll."

"Me too. Maybe that's what I'll have tonight."

"Sing a few bars of 'The Whiffenpoof Song' while you're there."

"Sissy's the singer."

"She was terrific in the senior production of *The Sound of Music*."

"So I hear. Wish I'd been there to see the play."

"Yes, we miss you."

"How's your campaign going?"

"Now that I have competition, we're stepping up the game. More yard signs, a few extra billboards, maybe some radio ads."

"Sissy said you're going to hire a plane to do sky writing."

"Ben and Edgar are pushing for that."

"Is Mr. Wurgler giving you a run for the money?"

"Nothing so far but a few debates."

"You can handle that. Weren't you a debate champion when you were here at Yale?"

"Back in the Dark Ages. But not to worry, Ken Wurgler couldn't talk his way out of a paper bag."

"That's f'sure. When he did job fairs at the high school, he'd get all mush-mouthed and at a loss for words."

"I don't think I have much to worry about."

"By the way, what's the latest on that clown's death?"

"You're asking me? I would've thought your Grammy had filled you in. She probably knows more than I do."

"I thought Uncle Jim kept you in the loop."

"He does, but it hard to keep up with your grandmother and her pals."

"Oh Dad, the Quilters Club is just trying to help out."

"I know, I know. That's why I made a deal with them on this one."

"What kinda deal?"

"That if I let them in, this would be their last case."

"Dad, you can't do that. N'yen and Sissy are part of the Quilters Club. Me too."

"Your cousin N'yen has never made a patchwork quilt in his life. Besides, you guys are in college or about to go. Your sleuthing careers are behind you."

"Don't be so sure about that," said Aggie. "We may surprise you."

CHAPTER FIFTY-TWO

The Car Wreck

Bootsie was on her way home from Strays & Rescues, just approaching the curve onto the Highway 21 Bypass, when her brakes went out. The pedal was suddenly mushy, slamming against the floorboard with a metallic *klunk*! She let out a loud shriek.

Her Subaru Impreza Hatchback took the curve too fast, its wheels losing traction. The magnetite gray SUV jumped the curb, plunging into the thicket of Squire Boone Jr. Forest, that patch of woods backing the Caruthers High football field. Branches and tree limbs slapped against the windshield. The seat felt like a rocking horse. The airbags deployed with the sound of an exploding grenade – *ka-pop*!

"Oh my, oh my, oh my," screamed Bootsie.

The car flipped.

She found herself hanging upside down, suspended in the air by nylon stands of the seatbelt. She was cocooned by airbags. Her leg hurt. She felt woozy. A siren wailed in the distance.

Then everything went black.

When she woke up, she was in a hospital bed.

~ ~ ~

"Somebody cut the brake line," said Buddy Flynn, wiping his greasy hands on his coveralls. He had towed the wrecked Subaru to his Texaco station out on Highway 21. "You can see it here, a clean slice with no ragged edges."

"Dang, who woulda done that?" said Deputy Tommy Truehart.

"Well, she *is* the police chief's wife," pointed out Buddy. "Not everybody likes what you lawmen do."

"Mostly we give out parking tickets."

"People don't like getting tickets. You know that."

"But why not go after us rather than the Chief's wife?"

Buddy Flynn shrugged. "Hard to fathom the criminal mind."

"You oughta, Buddy. You've done a stint in jail. And your brother's still doing hard time."

"Never mind that," the mechanic frowned. "All I'm saying is this wreck was not an accident."

CHAPTER FIFTY-THREE

Not an Accident

You're sure you're okay?" asked Jim Purdue. Standing next to Bootsie's hospital bed, he looked totally discombobulated. His bald pate was shiny. His eyes wide. His life revolved around his wife of over 40 years. Her leg was covered in a plaster cast, hoisted in a sling, like an elaborate Erector set. The white surface of the plaster was already defaced with scrawled autographs of her Quilters Club friends. Her bed was surrounded by colorful flowers – yellow and pink carnations. These were from Jim.

"Of course, I am. The Subaru ranks as one of the safest cars on the market. It's built with a solid frame designed to withstand collisions. I've seen crash test videos."

"Dear, you didn't collide with another car. Someone cut your brake line, according to Buddy Flynn. You ran off the road."

"And I collided with a tree. Where the airbag hit me in the chest hurts more than this stupid leg."

"The doctors say you'll be able to go home tomorrow. But you'll be confined to a wheelchair till that leg heals. That may take 3 to 6 months."

"Bah. I've got more interviews to do for the Quilters Club."

"That's not gonna happen. The girls can carry on without you – at least till that leg gets better. Doctors say you broke the fibula, a clean snap. But it could of been worse. You could of broke your neck."

Bootsie waved away his dire warnings. "Was the car totaled?"

"Yep. But don't worry about that. The insurance company will replace it. Maybe we'll get you a red one this time. The dealer over in Burpyville just got in a new truckload."

"Kinda feels like an early Christmas."

"If you say so. But Santa didn't sabotage your brake line. I'm thinking maybe it was a clown with green hair."

"Dear, we've eliminated all the clowns. It's gotta be someone else."

"Yes and no. I just learned that Mac Braselton used to be a clown in his early carny days. Tommy Truehart found a Wikipedia listing. Mac used to play a clown called Broccoli Top. That sounds like green hair to me."

~ ~ ~

Headed back to school, N'yen missed all the excitement. Apparently the telescope was back in operation. Classes resumed tomorrow.

And Sissy had embarked on an unexpected road trip with her grandfather. Buck had learned that Sissy's mother was being released from a rehab facility and was driving down to Alabama to pick her up. The plan was for her live with him and her daughter in Caruthers Corners. Everyone was nervous about that.

Aggie was prepared to fly home, but her Aunt Bootsie talked her out of it, assuring her that the broken leg was already on the mend. "See you at Christmas," Bootsie said, sounding chipper.

The other members of the Quilters Club were being extra cautious, not sure whether they were on some kind of "hit list" or not. Beau had wanted to hire a bodyguard for Maddy, but she refused to allow it.

~ ~ ~

"A dead end," replied Lizzie when Bootsie told her friends about her husband's new theory. They were all gathered around Bootsie's hospital bed, like mourners awaiting someone to administer the Last Rites. But their friend was actually feeling better, now that the pain medication was kicking in.

"How's it a dead end?"

"Mac Braselton was operating the Ferris wheel that evening," explained Lizzie. "Hundreds of people saw him. No way he was running around in a clown suit, green hair or not."

"Back to square one then," sighed Bootsie.

"Maybe not," said Maddy. "We now have a new line of investigation, thanks to someone cutting your brake line. That was likely Barffy's killer who did it. Perhaps we're getting too close for his comfort."

"We are?"

"Maybe he thinks so."

"How are you going to find this person who tampered with my car?"

"The brakes gave out on your way home," Maddy explained her line of thinking. "So the line must have been cut shortly before. It would take a few minutes for the brake fluid to drain."

"My car was parked at Strays & Rescues all morning," said Bootsie. "We were preparing a shipment of kittens for Chicago. There's a big demand for adoptions up there."

"That means your car was parked in one of the staff spaces. Isn't that covered by a security camera?"

Bootsie bobbed her pixie-style hair in the affirmative. "Should be. There's a camera mounted near the door. Can someone check it? Maybe we got the culprit on video."

Maddy said, "Who can do that?"

"Call Tommy Truehart. He's the one who installed the system."

CHAPTER FIFTY-FOUR

The Flying Floyds

That next morning, Det. Harry Teague drove over to Geneva to interview Jason Jonathan Floyd. The Floyd family still lived in the town where they had been born. Geneva (pop. 1,293) is a small town with historic charm. With many Old Order Amish and Swiss Mennonite families, it was named after Geneva, Switzerland.

The Floyds – widowed Jason Jonathan and his three grown children – shared a two-story clapboard farmhouse. A large barn out back held a trapeze rig where they practiced rigorously. The two boys sometimes joined the act, but daughter Priscilla was clearly the breakout star.

"What's up?" Jason Jonathan greeted the policeman.

"More questions about Barffy the Clown. Trying to piece together the timeline."

"Anything we can do to help, just ask."

"Thanks. Tried to call you but didn't get an answer."

"We turn off the phone when we're practicing. Don't want any sudden distractions when we're up there on the trapeze."

"Makes sense."

"You said you have questions?"

"Just a couple." Harry Teague turned to the daughter. "I understand you went to the restroom just before the show started."

"Yes, but how in the world did you know that? Don't tell me there was a surveillance camera in there."

"One of the other performers mentioned it. Did anyone see you go in the restroom?"

"No. Wait – yes! There was a ditzy old lady in there washing her hands. She said she'd just seen John Ringling North backstage. I figured she was nuts."

Harry grinned. "That would be Birdie Longstreet. Nuts pretty well sums it up."

"Nonetheless, I'm sure she would remember me. She thought I was Amelia Earhart."

"How about you, Mr. Floyd? Did you go anywhere before the show started?"

"Yeah, I went back to our dressing room for some chalk."
"Chalk?"

"That's right, I usually chalk up before a performance. Hands are everything. Caring for your hands will prevent rips and keep you swinging on a trapeze bar. It's important to build up calluses. Building calluses is a lot like building muscle. Breaking down the tissue and then rebuilding it stronger. The key is to trim, shave or buff that top layer of skin regularly to prevent tearing and build calluses under a deeper layer of skin. Then I tape my hands with athletic tape. Mueller's makes a great brand in a variety of fun colors – hot pink is my daughter's fave."

Priscilla smiled wryly. "Dad always says, 'A circus hurts; suck it up or take an art class.' Problem was, I couldn't draw a straight line. So I wear my circus scars and calluses proudly."

"That's my girl," smiled Jason Jonathan Floyd.

"So, Mr. Floyd, the only place you went was your dressing room?"

"No, after I chalked up and taped my hands, I stepped over to Walt Bradford's dressing room. It was next door to ours."

"Oh, was he there?"

"Yes, he was there with his manager, Col. Owensby. Walt was getting dressed. Putting on his greasepaint. Primping it up. I always thought he was more drag queen than clown."

"Why did you go over?"

"I wanted to give him a piece of my mind. He'd been hitting on Prissy during rehearsal. I wanted to tell him to lay off."

"Did you?"

"No, I didn't want to say anything in front of Col. Owensby."

"So you left?"

"Right. Merely told him to bump a nose and left."

"Do what?"

"Bump a nose. That's clown speak for good luck."

"Was he wearing his red nose when you saw him?"

Jason Jonathan Floyd paused to picture the scene in his mind's eye. "No, he wasn't. It was laying there in front of him on the dressing table."

"Was there anything written on his mirror at that time?"

"No."

"Did you have an apple in your hand?"

"An apple? No."

"Someone saw you in Clown Alley with something round and red in your hand. A clown's nose perhaps?"

"Oh, you must mean my roll of tape. It's a reddish. Was probably that weird guy with three eyes who saw me. He's a headliner at the Freak Show, I believe."

"Yes. Anybody else see you?"

"Well, Col. Owensby and Barffy."

"And you say Col. Owensby can attest that you merely stuck your head in the dressing room, wished Barffy good luck, then left."

"That's right. But I didn't mean it."

"Didn't mean what?"

"I didn't really mean for him to have good luck."

"Well, he didn't."

~ ~ ~

"Nothing here," said Tommy. The deputy had checked the video camera trained on the Strays & Rescues parking lot. He offered an apologetic shrug.

"Why not?" asked his boss. Chief Purdue had gone over to the animal shelter with him to see if the surveillance system had captured the image of some interloper crawling under his wife's Subaru to cut through the brake line, allowing the fluid to drain out.

"Nobody turned on the system. So the camera didn't record anything."

"Well, that's a fine how-do-you-do." But the police chief didn't push it. He knew it was his wife's technological naïveté at fault. She was always forgetting to lock the door, activate the surveillance system, turn off the lights.

"We struck out here," admitted Tommy, "but I have another idea. Let's check out Wabash Acres. The development has its own security system. I installed it too. One of the cameras at the front gate angles in this direction. Maybe it will give us a hint about the traffic visiting the animal shelter yesterday morning."

"Deputy Truehart, you may earn yourself an accommodation yet."

"A raise would be better," he mumbled.

CHAPTER FIFTY-FIVE

Out-of-Towner

Tommy leaned close to the flickering video screen, his nose practically brushing the glass surface. He and Chief Purdue were hunkered in the tiny security room of Wabash Acres, a low-income retirement development on Highway 21. The room was barely bigger than a closet, crammed with video equipment. "Here you go, a car turning into Strays & Rescues. Time, 10:47 A.M."

"How do you know this is the one? Could be a volunteer. Or somebody dropping off a stray kitten. Or looking to adopt a dog."

"Because this is a rental car – see that barcode sticker on the window. And it has an Illinois license plate with an FP on it. That's a Fleet Permanent plate like rental companies use in Illinois."

"You think someone rented a car in Illinois to drive down here and sabotage my wife's car?"

"That's exactly what I'm thinking. Didn't those clown car clowns come from Chicago? Bet it's one of them. Doubt any of them own a vehicle other than that stupid clown car or a van with their name painted on the side. Nothing you'd want to be seen in if you were planning on cutting someone's brake line."

Jim Purdue rubbed his hand over the sweaty dome of his head. "But they all had alibies."

"Maybe we oughta take a closer look at them alibies."

~ ~ ~

Entertainment booker Eric J. Littleton knew his Klown Kar Krew were low-lifes who worked as circus clowns because no hard labor was involved. They were mostly lazy louts who existed on drinking beer and playing poker in their spare time. And they had lots of spare time between bookings. The circus business – including carnivals, county fairs, corporate events, and birthday parties – was drying up. Clowns were going the way of the dodo. But, being at the end of his career, Littleton would keep them as clients until the bitter end.

Unfortunately, the bitter end seemed nigh.

Knowing his clients, he wouldn't trust them with pocket change. The Klown Kar Krew was an unruly, dishonest, dangerous group. He was sure they were lying to those investigators, alibiing each other. They would do that out of habit, whether they had something to hide or not.

Should he give that police detective a heads-up? Should he forewarn those women who came poking around? Or should he mind his own business?

He opted for the latter. Billy Tuckman was a mean sonuvagun. He might just cut your throat if you crossed him. At Eric Littleton's advanced age, he didn't need any trouble.

~ ~ ~

"Heard back from Enterprise, the rental car company whose car we caught on video," reported Deputy Tommy

Truehart. "It was rented with a MasterCard belonging to Klown Kar Krew Inc. I think we're closing in on a suspect."

"Who used the card?"

"That's the problem. Enterprise can't tell me. At least not yet. They've had a system meltdown. Got their IP people working on it. The supervisor I spoke with hopes to be back up by tomorrow."

"What rotten luck. But stay on it, Tommy. I want that name."

~ ~ ~

Det. Teague phoned in from Geneva. "Both Floyd and his daughter checked out. I believe their stories. He left Barffy with Col. Owensby. The nose hadn't been put on yet. But hard to tell who might have had access to it before then to put ricin powder in it."

"We've gotta think this through," said Chief Purdue. His voice sounded a million miles away over the phone.

"Why not call in the Quilters Club. Your wife and her friends are pretty good at sniffing things out."

"Sniffing," said the Chief. "That's what did Barffy in."

"That's a true fact."

"Okay, come on home. Let's have everybody meet first thing tomorrow morning at the police department. Quilters Club too. We're gonna solve this sucker even if it takes their help!"

CHAPTER FIFTY-SIX

The Timeline

Here's the timeline best we know it," said Maddy Madison, standing before a green-slated chalk board in the police station's cramped interrogation room. Harry Teague had dragged the chalkboard into the room especially for this meeting. He had found an eraser, but was now searching for an unbroken stick of chalk. Unable to find one, he handed Maddy a stubby piece about the size of a 9mm bullet.

Maddy began writing on the dusty green surface:

5:00 "The Come In," the period before showtime when audience enter the arena.

5:30 Circus performers begin gathering in waiting area outside main ring. Half hour to showtime. (Barffy not there yet.)

5:35 Priscilla goes to restroom, spots Birdie.

5:40 Priscilla returns to waiting area.

5:42 Floyd chalks and wraps hands in his own dressing room.

5:43 Floyd encounters Three Eyes wandering around Clown Alley. (Floyd is carrying roll of tape.)

5:45 Floyd sees Barffy in dressing room with Manager. (Barffy not wearing poisoned nose yet.)

5:47 Floyd returns to waiting area.

5:50 Barffy arrives at waiting area. Ten minutes to showtime. (Barffy now wearing poisoned nose.)

5:52 Sprinkles enters dressing room. (Barffy was already at ringside wearing poisoned nose.)

5:53 Birdie encounters Sprinkles in dressing room. (Sprinkles is writing on mirror.)

5:54 Wanda spots Three Eyes crawling under tent. (Three Eyes looking to steal something.)

5:55 Three Eyes spots Birdie and Sprinkles in dressing room.

5:56 Three Eyes quickly exits dressing room.

5:57 Birdie exits dressing room (after being threatened by Sprinkles.)

5:59 Sprinkles exits dressing room (after writing on mirror.)

6:00 Barffy begins the opening act (wearing poisoned nose).

6:15 Barffy dies during his act (wearing poisoned nose).

"A timeline – does this look about right?" she asked. "Times are approximate, but in the right order I think."

Everybody leaned forward to study the board – the Chief, Harry, Tommy, the other members of the Quilters Club (including Bootsie in a BLS18FBD-ELR Blue Streak Lightweight Wheelchair with an elevated leg rest for her plaster cast).

Chief Purdue was the first to speak. "Well, this would eliminate Jason Jonathan Floyd and his daughter," he observed. "They have witnesses to verify where they were when not waiting outside the ring. They didn't have an opportunity to doctor Barffy's rubber nose. Barffy's manager was there in the room with him."

"And Bobby Ray, Birdie, and Three Eyes can alibi each other," Harry Teague pointed out. "They didn't have access to the nose. Barffy had already gone to the waiting area with his poisoned nose before the trio met up in his dressing room."

"Well, that clears the clown with green hair," sighed Jim Purdue with an air of disappointment.

Lizzie said, "What about Three Eyes' claim that he saw Floyd with a rubber nose?"

"Even with three eyes, his eyesight is pretty poor," countered Tommy Truehart. "I'm not sure we can put much stock in what he said he saw."

"It was probably the roll of tape, like Floyd said," nodded Chief Purdue. "So let's set his story aside for a moment."

"What about them clown car yahoos?" asked Tommy. "We know one of them was involved in Mrs. Purdue's accident, so why not poisoning Barffy too?"

"Problem is, they all have alibis for the carnival. One of them cut that brake line, but he didn't get at Barffy's rubber nose. That had to be someone else."

"So who poisoned Barffy?"

"Beats me," said the Police Chief. "We've accounted for everybody."

"Not everybody," said Maddy.

"Oh, who else?"

"What about Col. Owensby?" she responded. "We know he was with Barffy around 5:45, but what if he got there earlier, before Barffy. That would give him a chance to dose that red nose with the poison."

"Barffy's manager? What motivation would he have had?" challenged Bootsie. "Barffy was his meal ticket."

"Wait a sec," said Cookie. "Didn't that Chicago booker say Barffy was thinking of retiring?"

"Yes," nodded Lizzie. "That's what Mr. Littleton told Sissy. He was lamenting the loss of income that would've caused."

"Dying causes a loss of income too," argued Bootsie.

"So how does that help Col. Owensby?" asked Deputy Truehart. Confused by all the back-and-forth.

Maddy summed it up. "Like my grandson N'yen said before – who benefits? I'd bet the Colonel has a fat insurance policy on his deceased client."

CHAPTER FIFTY-SEVEN

Wrapping It Up

Tommy Truehart used his computer wizardry to search for any recent insurance applications by Col. Owensby. He turned up one on the third try. Two million bucks with Lloyd's of London. The insurance company has covered many famous people's attributes – Tina Turner's legs, J-Lo's backside, Gene Simmons' tongue, Tom Jones's chest hair. Even a monkey that was a key player in a Vaudeville act. Barffy and his red nose had been a no-brainer.

~ ~ ~

Harry Teague drove to Chicago to make another run at the Klown Kar Krew. They all alibied each other, but what if they were lying? After all, one of them had sabotaged Bootsie Purdue's car. Something was going on there.

So he was going to push even harder.

At the detective's request, Eric J. Littleton had gathered all twelve of his clown car clients into his small conference room. It was almost like crowding them into the Fiat 500 used in their act.

"Anybody lying's gonna be charged with obstruction," announced Harry Teague to the assemblage. "First one speaks up gets a free pass. Everybody else will face charges. Do we understand each other?"

Green Grasshopper was the first to break. "Okay, we're covering for Billy. He's our chum. But I'm not gonna take a fall for him. I don't wanna be accused of murder, just because my clown face has green hair."

"Where was Billy Tuckman prior to Barffy's performance that night?" Harry and Gary Griffin had stepped out of the conference room for a one-on-one chat. Each man was getting a private turn with the detective, a chance to spill the beans.

"Billy swears he went to take a leak, but I know he's not telling the truth. He has this little tic under his left eye when he's lying. I like playing cards with him because he can never bluff."

"Guess I better have another conversation with Billy Boy," said the detective. "As Ricky Ricardo used to say to Lucy, there's some 'splaining to do."

~ ~ ~

"Billy Tuckman was the green-haired clown in Barffy's dressing room," confirmed Harry Teague, phoning in from Chicago.

"Do we need to extradite him from Illinois? If so, I'll get Judge Cramer to start the paperwork."

"No need. He's volunteered to come back with me. Confessed everything."

"Everything?"

"Well, not the murder. But he admits he's the guy who cut Bootsie's brakes. And the clown who wrote on the mirror."

"Then that means Bobby Ray was lying," said the Chief.

"Yeah, but why would he do that?"

"My cousin's got more money than brains. Hard to tell why he does anything."

~ ~ ~

"Billy Tuckman admitted he was the guy who cut your break line," Jim Purdue told his wife. "You spooked him when you confronted him in Chicago, so he decided to get rid of you. He didn't know you were working with your Quilters Club friends or he would have went after them too."

"What about Barffy's death?" asked Maddy. "Was he in on that?"

"He fingered Col. Owensby as the man who hired him to write that message on the mirror. But he claims he didn't know the Colonel planned to kill Barffy."

"I suspect he's lying about that," said Maddy.

"Why's that?" frowned Bootsie.

"Because he wouldn't have tried to kill you otherwise. Writing on a mirror isn't serious enough for that."

"So we agree Col. Owensby put the ricin in Barffy's rubber nose?" said Lizzie.

"Had to be him," nodded Cookie. "Like our timetable proved, nobody else had the access to do it."

"There's no doubt the Colonel's our man," nodded Chief Purdue. "Guess we better pick him up. I sure hope he hasn't left town yet."

"Not yet," called Tommy Truehart from his desk in the next room. The police department was small and crowded, the deputies used to calling out to each other from room to room. "But you'd better hurry. He's about to fly the coop."

"What's that you say?"

"An Oscar Otis Owensby's booked on a 3:30 flight out of Burpyville Regional."

"How d'you know that?"

"Says so right here," Tommy waved at his computer screen. "I'm hacked into the reservation system of Hoosier Express Airlines."

"Don't tell me that," groaned Chief Purdue.

"He's already checked in."

"Then we'd better get a move on," said Jim Purdue. "You want to ride down to Burpyville with me, Tommy?"

"Sure," the deputy nodded. Seeing this as a reward for his good work. Hacking or not.

"Bring your cuffs."

CHAPTER FIFTY-EIGHT

Confession

Police Chief Jim Purdue sat across the interrogation-room table from Col. Oscar Owensby. They had picked up Owensby at the Burpyville Regional Airport just before he boarded a flight with connections to Florida. That was a stroke of luck, for extraditions from other states were a pain in the keister. Lots of paperwork and lost time.

"Me kill Barffy? That's outrageous," the clown's manager had protested.

"According to reliable sources, you have a two-million-dollar policy on Walter Ambrose Bradford with Lloyd's of London. That's a pretty good motive for murder," stated Chief Purdue.

"So what? It's common practice to insure your clients. It's like 'key man' insurance in a big company."

"There's more," said Jim Purdue. "As you know, we exercised a search warrant for your laptop computer. Duly signed this afternoon by Judge Horace Cramer. My deputy Tommy Truehart here is a computer whiz. He found that you recently conducted Google searches for WHAT'S A FAST-ACTING POISON? WHICH POISON IS HARD TO DETECT? And WHERE CAN I BUY CASTOR-OIL BEANS? That's pretty damning, wouldn't you say?"

"Mere curiosity."

"Prior to your client dying by exactly those means?"

"Coincidence."

"Well, here's a coincidence for you. Sweet Pea the Clown – better known as William Charles Tuckman, boss of the Klown Kar Krew – has admitted that you paid him $2,000 to sneak into Barffy's dressing room and write a threating note on the mirror. He said it was to throw suspicion off you."

"He can't prove that. I paid him in cash." The Colonel paused to consider what he'd just said. "Oops," he added.

"Thank you for that confession," concluded Chief Purdue, clicking off the tape recorder.

CHAPTER FIFTY-NINE

Bobby Ray's Big Lie

Bobby Ray Purdue said, "Okay, I lied. I didn't go to the carnival in my clown costume. That was just a story I told Molly Connell to impress her. We were having dinner at Cozy Café 'cause it was close to home. I confess I had seduction in mind. She's a very attractive young woman."

"Molly Connell? Isn't she that new singer?"

"Yep. Her song *Be My Boyfriend Tonight* was Number One on the charts last week. Guess I was applying for the position."

Chief Purdue frowned. "How did you know about the message on the mirror and Birdie Longstreet being there?"

"Tommy Truehart told me. My Internet went down and I hired Tommy to come fix it. He moonlights as an IP techie. The boy's good. I asked him about the clown's death and he told me he'd just interviewed Birdie. He thought she was imagining the whole thing – seeing clowns in Barffy's dressing room."

"Turns out, she did see two 'clowns' – but they were Billy Tuckman and Three Eyes Johnson. You weren't there at all."

"Hey, you can't blame me for trying to impress Molly. She's gorgeous, a talented singer, and single. I met her through Lucius Plancus – she's his second cousin."

"Lucius Plancus, that WZUR reporter?"

"Right, the one they call The Jolly Red Giant. Molly is from Pitsville too. Won a talent contest, signed a recording contract, now living it large with a hit record. Guess I was trying hard to impress her."

"Your millions of dollars didn't impress her?"

"I want people to like me for who I am, not my money."

"But you weren't who you said you were, the clown who wrote on Barffy's mirror."

"Minor detail."

"Then why did you tell Maddy Madison that you were there and met up with Birdie?"

"I was just talking. Didn't see any harm in it."

"You almost got yourself arrested for murder."

~ ~ ~

"So, did Bobby Ray succeed in seducing Molly Connell?" Aggie asked when her grandmother repeated the story. Their Sunday night calls were as regular as clockwork. 8 o'clock on the dot, 9 Eastern Standard Time.

"Young lady, that is not a topic for you."

"Grammy, I'm in college. I know people have sex."

"Yes, but *I* don't want to know that you know."

Maddy could hear the girl chuckle over the phone. "I'll bet Aunt Lizzie asked the same question."

"Matter of fact, she did. But you know she lives for every episode of *Entertainment Tonight* and the next issue of *People Weekly*. The woman thrives on gossip."

"Molly Connell's a big deal. Everybody says she's sure to win a Grammy as this year's Best New Artist."

"There's an award for that?"

"Yes, the award for Best New Artist has been presented since the 2nd Annual Grammy Awards in 1960. Molly Connell has been getting lots of good buzz. I'd say she's a lock."

"N'yen's coming back next weekend. He and Sissy are putting up yard signs for your dad's campaign."

"Wish I could be there to help them."

"You stay and study. Those little lovebirds don't need a third wheel," Maddy teased.

"I suppose that's true. I miss when we were all a team, part of the Quilters Club solving mysteries."

"We all need to be moving on," sighed Maddy. "Me and the gals aren't spring chickens anymore. And you kids are moving ahead with your own lives. In a few more years you'll be a lawyer, probably working for – what do they call it? – a white shoe law firm in a big city. You will be fighting crime and solving mysteries in your own way."

"Or maybe I'll come home and open up a law firm in Caruthers Corners. The town could use another good attorney."

"Oh?"

"Maybe by then my Daddy will have retired from politics and want to have a partner in a new law firm. Tidemore & Tidemore has a nice ring to it, don't you think?"

CHAPTER SIXTY

Election Day

That Tuesday in November the good citizens of Caruthers Corners turned out to vote. Early reports confirmed that it was going to be a landslide for Mark Tidemore. By 4 o'clock, long before the polls had closed, Ken Wurgler gave a concession speech.

"Thank you for your support," he said. However, the voters had offered very little.

Mark followed that with a statement that he was looking forward to another four years as the town's mayor. "Now back to work," he concluded.

As it turned out, Ben Bentley only put out $7,312 – far short of his $50,000 pledge – most of the funds spent again this year on yard signs and billboards. A plane doing sky writing was canceled at the last minute. Bobby Ray Purdue got away without writing a single check. Promotions were pulled back when they saw that Ken Wurgler wasn't even going for yard signs. Bobby Ray agreed to donate the money to the town.

~ ~ ~

"Congratulations, Dad," said Aggie. She was calling that night from New Haven. She had been prepared to fly home to vote, but her father – good at reading the political climate – assured her it wasn't necessary.

You have to be 18 to vote in Indiana, so Aggie qualified; but N'yen and Sissy did not. Nevertheless, her cousin and her bestie had worked tirelessly putting up hundreds of yard signs. Now that N'yen had a car, they could make better progress, his Beetle crawling down the street while Sissy ran door-to-door asking if they could place a sign in the front yard.

The backseat of the little VW had been piled high with printed placards and sharp wooden stakes. It was nearly as crowded as that Krazy Klown car that was supposed to be part of the entertainment at the recent carnival.

"Thanks, dear. Are you coming home for Christmas? Your mom could use a visit."

Aggie's mom was recovering from a long mental funk in which she fantasized about fairies and dragons and unicorns. Hypnotic therapy had helped bring her back to the real world. They owed The Great Wizardini for that bit of real magic. Maybe that's why her Grammy went so easy on Dorothy and her parents.

"I'll be there," Aggie promised. "Tige is coming back to school with me. I just put a deposit on a new pet-friendly apartment." Each of Maddy's grandchildren having a trust fund, Aggie could make these choices without asking her parents for money.

"How does your Grammy feel about giving up Tige?"

"I'm sure she will miss him, but he *is* my dog."

"True enough."

"I've promised to bring Tige to visit every time I come home."

"She'll like that, I'm sure."

"But I can't take him to Pleasant Glade."

"Why's that?"

"No dogs allowed in the boneyard," she repeated her Grammy's childhood mantra.

"Sweetie, there's actually no law against dogs in the cemetery."

"Are you sure."

"Of course. I'm the mayor."

EPILOGUE

Maddy Madison and the Quilters Club took no credit for solving what *Burpyville Gazette* had dubbed "The Killer Clown Case." They knew when to fade into the background and let the Caruthers Corners Police Department take a bow. After all, Chief Jim Purdue and Doc Medford played a major role in solving the crime too.

Cooperation, that had been the key.

Judge Cramer presided over the trial. Col. Oscar Otis Owensby was sentenced to 30 years in prison. That was likely a life sentence for a man of his age. Billy Tuckman – A/K/A Sweet Pea the Clown – got 10 years as an Accessory After the Fact. Turns out, the Colonel also had promised to take over Tuckman's management. But that wouldn't be happening.

The Klown Kar Krew was making do with 11 bozos stuffed into the kandy-kolored tangerine-flake streamline Fiat 500. Nobody had liked Billy that much anyway. Green Grasshopper became the new Boss Clown. The police dropped any obstruction charges.

Newly re-elected Mayor Mark Tidemore presented Beatrice Longstreet with a gold-plated Distinguished Citizen medal for her report of the clown she saw writing on the mirror, the incident that "cracked the case" according to the front-page article that appeared in the *Burpyville Gazette*.

Birdie thought the medal was for her flower garden, a bed of roses which she had planted as part of the town's Beautification Program.

The Great Wizardini and Mary Alice Hegler elected to keep their true relationship a secret. They preferred the status quo. And Dorothy Starcatcher chose not to reveal her parentage – though rumors still circulated. The Quilters Club (both senior and junior members) agreed to keep the facts to themselves. So far, Lizzie hasn't said a word.

Ken Wurgler retired from his position as president of the Caruthers Corners Chamber of Commerce and moved to Florida. That was the deal for overlooking his financial irregularities. Ken considered his run for mayor the conclusion to his political career. He'd received 32 votes out of 1,312 cast in the recent election. The constituency had spoken. To heck with them!

The $92,688 unspent campaign funds went toward losses from the Crazy Carnival. Gimble & Gimble were retained to plan another carnival for next September. Topsy the Clown would headline. He had joined a 12-step program. The Klown Kar Krew had been booked, too.

Aggie took her dog Tige back to New Haven. Beau got the family a new puppy, a beagle from Judge Cramer. He named him Mutt.

With Sissy receiving the original Crazy Carnival Quilt, and the Heglers getting a duplicate, the Quilters Club set aside their Crazy Quilts project and began work on a third Crazy Carnival Quilt commissioned by the Town. It would hang in the lobby of the Town Hall until next year when it would be auctioned off prior to the next circus event.

Maddy Madison announced that the Quilters Club was retiring from its detective work, "from now on sticking to patchwork quilts."

But her granddaughter Aggie had other ideas.

Thank you for reading.
Please review this book. Reviews
help others find Absolutely Amazing eBooks and
inspire us to keep providing these marvelous tales.
If you would like to be put on our email list
to receive updates on new releases,
contests, and promotions, please go to
AbsolutelyAmazingEbooks.com and sign up.

ABOUT THE AUTHOR

Marjory Sorrell Rockwell says needlecraft arts – quilting, crocheting, knitting – are pastimes every woman can appreciate. And she particularly loves quiltmaking. "It's like painting with cloth," she says. But when not quilting she writes mysteries about a Midwestern sleuth not unlike herself, a middle-aged lady with an unpredictable family and loyal friends. And she's a big fan of watermelon pie.

Quilter Club Mysteries

Visit Maddy's new website...

quiltersclubmysteries.com/

Take a tour of Caruthers Corners and the surrounding countryside. Meet Maddy's family and friends. Get a complete list of all the characters who have appeared in the entire Quilters Club Mysteries book series. Well, practically all.

What's more, you'll learn lots about quilting. There's a free quilt pattern. A dictionary of quilting terms. Even a Quilt Gallery showing some of Maddy's favorite quilt patterns.

No fees, no charges. Just fun.

For sales, editorial information, subsidiary rights information
or a catalog, please write or phone or e-mail
AbsolutelyAmazingEbooks
Manhanset House
Shelter Island Hts., New York 11965-0342, US
Tel: 212-427-7139
www.AbsolutelyAmazingEbooks.com
bricktower@aol.com
www.IngramContent.com

For sales in the UK and Europe please contact our distributor,
Gazelle Book Services
White Cross Mills
Lancaster, LA1 4XS, UK
Tel: (01524) 68765 Fax: (01524) 63232
email: jacky@gazellebooks.co.uk

www.ingramcontent.com/pod-product-compliance
Lightning Source LLC
Chambersburg PA
CBHW071835020726
47502CB00004B/1369